W9-AHF-418

The legend of Crazy Woman Canyon

The legend of Crazy Woman Canyon

Second Edition

Dr. Gary L. Morris

Copyright © 2012 by Dr. Gary L. Morris.

ISBN: Softcover   978-1-4797-2904-3
                Ebook   978-1-4797-2905-0

All rights reserved. No part of this book may be reproduced or transmitted in any form or by any means, electronic or mechanical, including photocopying, recording, or by any information storage and retrieval system, without permission in writing from the copyright owner.

This is a work of fiction. Names, characters, places and incidents either are the product of the author's imagination or are used fictitiously, and any resemblance to any actual persons, living or dead, events, or locales is entirely coincidental.

This book was printed in the United States of America.

To order additional copies of this book, contact:
Xlibris Corporation
1-888-795-4274
www.Xlibris.com
Orders@Xlibris.com
123761

Contents

DEDICATION

This story is dedicated to my great aunt Lucy McGrath who made great roast pork and lima beans but whose life still remains a mystery to me, to my dad Charles Leon Morris, who neither pushed nor pulled me, to my mother Esther Grace Balden who loves me, to my wife Lia who nurtures me, to my daughters Pamela, Deborah, Cynthia, and Linda who understand me, to history that instructs me, and to the Native Americans who give me hope that our planet will survive.

Author's Note

There is a very nice museum located in Buffalo, Wyoming that is visited by thousands of tourists annually. Since the town of Buffalo is located on a major highway midway between Mount Rushmore and Yellowstone Park, many people stop there for a breather—spending several hours in the museum, in the city park with its beautiful mature cottonwood trees and free Olympic-sized outdoor swimming pool, or just walking around town looking at all the old western storefronts and souvenir shops. Some travelers even decide to stay overnight at the historic Occidental Hotel and dine at the Virginian Restaurant. The locals are friendly and love to tell their stories of local lore to any tourist who will listen. They also enjoy telling the tourists about their favorite nature haunts that are located within an hour or so drive from Buffalo. Invariably, Crazy Woman Canyon is mentioned as a must see. The mouth of the canyon is located some 15 miles from Buffalo and the five mile drive up the breathtaking canyon takes between one and three hours depending on how many times one gets out of the car to take pictures, movies or just to walk and explore. I doubt than anyone, other than a local who actually drives the canyon on a daily basis to work or lives nearby, could drive up that canyon without taking at least one picture. It's one of the most beautiful places on earth. Without exception, each visitor to the canyon will rush back to town and ask a local, "Why is it called Crazy Woman Canyon?" Most times the local will say, "I don't know" and give the tourist a list of people to talk to who they say may know something about the canyon and a list of places in town to visit where the traveler might find these "fountains of knowledge". After the tourists had walked or driven all over town and had exhausted all the resources they had been given, to no avail, they would usually end up back at the museum bookstore. The first question on their lips would be, "Is there a book about how Crazy Woman Canyon got its name?" My own wife, incidentally, was one of those inquirers. The answer would be a simple, "No." There had never been a book written about how the famous canyon got its name—at least until now. I have attempted to shed some light or maybe some darkness on the problem. You, reader, may be the judge. In any case, now there is a book.

This book can not hope to impress the reader the way the natural grandeur and beauty of the canyon itself will impress the visitor, but I hope the reader will enjoy my tale and cherish it as a souvenir of their visit to the Buffalo area and the canyon on Crazy Woman Creek.

My tale is based on historical facts and is set in real places and times as much as is possible when spinning a tale about how a legend came to be. I have taken certain liberties with the deeds of various historical figures to add a little extra drama to my tale. I hope that their ghosts don't mind. The story may or may not have been told to my great aunt Lucy McGrath in the early 1920s by Manuela Lisa's granddaughter and I may or may not have found the manuscript written in Aunt Lucy's own hand along with the secret document mentioned in this tale when cleaning out my Dad's house in Buffalo, Wyoming. If my Dad could still speak, he would probably say, "That's a likely story." However, the story could be true. Who can say it's not? "Who knows? The Shadow knows, ha, ha, ha, ha, ha."

All things are bound together.
All things connect.
What happens to the earth happens to the children of the earth.

Chief Seattle, 1855

We must embrace this concept and act accordingly if we endeavor to survive as a species on this planet into the twenty-second century.

Doctor Gary Lee Morris, 2008

Introduction

My name is Manuela Lisa. I was born in St. Louis, Missouri, in 1809. My father, Manuel Lisa, was a Spaniard who had a reputation for being violent, ruthless and unprincipled. He was born in New Orleans, but after receiving a land grant, established a home in St. Louis in 1799. Prior to 1799 he had reportedly spied for anyone who would pay him, been involved with government contracts, bribery; and he had smuggled all manner of goods in and out of Santa Fe and New Orleans. He is noted in history books for outfitting the Louis and Clark Expedition and his involvement in the fur trade along the Missouri river. He was one of the first to employ white fur trappers instead of trading with the Indians for furs. These hardy white trappers became known as mountain men. The mountain men, both company men and independents, existed between about 1800 and 1850 but their heyday was between 1820 and 1835. The period of the mountain man seemed to have officially come to an end with the last rendezvous in 1838.

What follows is the short story of my life that began in St. Louis and ended in a small town located on the eastern foothills of the Bighorn Mountains. I will tell you about the town of my birth, how I came to travel west into the wilderness with some of the first mountain men, my involvement in fur trading and trapping, and relate to you some of the adventures I had there. Then, I will tell you about how I came to Wyoming Territory and some of the things that happened there, including how a creek, a crossing, a canyon, and a battlefield came to be named after me. Finally, I will tell you about my later years as an Indian Medicine Woman and the proprietor of a trading post on the Bozeman trail. I have chosen not to dwell too much on the negative, but there is certainly a lot of it. It was and still is, to a lesser extent now, a hard life in the Great Plains area of these United States. The story of "how the west was won" is as tragic as it is epic. The European Americans pushed west even as their nation was still young and they took what they wanted from the Native Americans—nearly exterminating all of them and their cultures as they went, much as the Spaniards and other Europeans had done in Mexico, Central and South America, and the islands of the Caribbean a few centuries before them. This is not a story of cowboys and Indians typical of the nineteenth and twentieth century stories of the Old West. It is a story of greed, achievement, hardship, conflict, survival, deceit, the beauty of the Indian culture, and the ugliness of early American politics—but mostly of greed.

Chapter One

The Fur Trade

The fur trade in North America began around 1600 when the French began the quest for beaver fur. The trade started in the area of what was to become Canada—later drifting down to the St. Laurence River to the Great Lakes Area. Some of these hardy fur traders stayed in the northern river systems and some went further south down the Mississippi River to where it joined the Missouri River and then followed the Missouri River west into the Rocky Mountains and into what would later become Wyoming Territory. Many of these early traders were the product of unions between French men and the Indian squaws who dwelt in the areas where the Frenchmen traded. These mixed bloods were called Métis. It was common in the first 220 years of the fur business for traders to take Indian wives partly because these squaws were very adept at finding, preparing, and preserving all manner of foods found in the wilderness, preparing beaver pelts for shipment, setting up and breaking up camp sites quickly, and using weapons when called upon to do so. Another good reason for taking a local Indian as one's wife was that her whole family, which sometimes consisted of an entire Indian village, would become customers of the trader—trading their pelts for such things as blankets, beads, and small iron axes (tomahawks).

The Métis lived among their full-blooded Indian neighbors and shared the customs, traditions, and religious practices of both the Indians and the French. The English and then the European American followed suit and also lived in general harmony with the Indians—trading with them and shipping their pressed pallets of beaver pelts to St. Louis and New Orleans. Everything seemed to be going well until after the Louisiana Purchase when more and more white men started permanently encroaching on Indian lands. The Indians did not mind a few traders who basically accepted and respected their way of life and even wedded their daughters, but they could not understand or abide the white man who wanted to acquire a piece of land, call it his own, and build a permanent residence on it.

In the early 1800's white settlers became too numerous, and Indian hunting grounds began to become depleted, causing trade agreements between the many fur traders and the Indians to break down. Many Indians would no longer trade their pelts with the white men but the demand for felt hats and beaver fur to make accessories for gentlemen's and ladies' clothing was greater than ever. That is when my father and a few others decided it was time for white men to venture into the western wilderness in greater numbers to trap the beaver themselves. The age of the Mountain Man was born.

Manuel Lisa made his home in St. Louis but he accompanied his trappers and traders far into the western lands and was able to secure cooperation from all manner of "Redskin" by plying them with trinkets and through his knowledge of their customs and their supposed idiosyncrasies. He established several forts along his trade routes including Fort Raymond, named after my brother, in what is now Montana, and Fort Lisa in what is now Nebraska. Although he had a wife in St. Louis, he had taken at least one Indian wife as well. My brother and I were the products of the union between our father and one of these Indian women who he later married in 1814. I had at least one other half-breed brother but I did not know this until I had ventured out west. In any case, after I was born, my father brought my mother, my brother, and me to St. Louis.

Chapter Two

St. Louis, the Gateway to the West

St. Louis was founded in 1763 near the mouth of the Missouri River. Once the town got established, it quickly became the worldwide center of the fur trade. In 1764 Pierre Laclede traveled upstream on the Mississippi River looking for a good spot to establish a post for trading with the Indians. St. Louis was a perfect location. One could enter the Missouri and Illinois Rivers and go north and west to trade with the Indians, float the goods, mainly beaver pelts, down the river to New Orleans, and ship them out to such places as London, Paris, and Amsterdam. In turn, one could float certain goods up the Mississippi River to St. Louis to be traded to the Indians. These shipments usually included firearms, wool blankets, glass beads, arrowheads, shells, and an iron mini-axe called the tomahawk. These tomahawks, so named because the curve of the metal blade looked like a hawk's beak, were very popular among the Indians and were mass-produced in France and shipped in great numbers to New Orleans, St. Louis and the areas where Indians trapped the beaver.

By 1787 there were more than 1,000 people living in St. Louis, but the transient population was much larger. There were banks, boarding houses, and bars lining the streets for two miles inland of the riverbanks. According to one historian St. Louis was a "noisy, smelly, violent and raucous place". On any given day, along the waterfront, one could see extravagant, boisterous Mississippi River boatmen; good natured, singing Canadian voyagers; vagrant Indians of several tribes, and Kentucky hunters clothed in buckskin, toting long rifles and large knives.

St. Louis became the capital of upper Louisiana in 1765 and was governed by a French lieutenant governor from 1766 to 1768. After 1768 Spanish authorities governed it even after its return to the French in 1800. After the Louisiana Purchase, St. Louis became a part of the United States, and it was incorporated as a town in 1809. By that time, I have been told, there were large warehouses along the docks that were used to store the beaver pelts and other furs and hides for shipment to New Orleans and other destinations. These shipments were made in river boats, but it typically took at least eight months to travel the 1,278 miles from St. Louis to New Orleans. The invention of the steamboat or paddle wheeler, as it was often called, in 1811 greatly decreased this time once these new boats started making the trip.

In 1817 the golden age of the paddle wheeler had begun. In 1814 there were 21 of these steamboats traveling out of New Orleans; in 1819 there were 191, and in 1833 there were more than 1,200. At first the steamboats traveled between New Orleans and Natchez, then they traveled between New Orleans and Louisville, then from New Orleans to St. Louis, and eventually from St. Louis as far north as St. Paul. The first paddle wheeler to make the entire trip from New Orleans to St. Louis was the *Zebulon M. Pike* in 1817, and it took about 40 days. In 1838 the same trip took about 12 days. Steamboat travel greatly enhanced the development of the fur trade and it increased the wealth of New Orleans and helped establish St. Louis as the worldwide capital of the fur trade and the capital of upper Louisiana. By 1830 steamboats were traveling north to the upper Mississippi, and by 1840 there was heavy steamboat traffic between St. Louis and St. Paul.

Paddle wheel steamboats continued to develop after the middle part of the nineteenth century. They became larger, more powerful, and more luxurious. Initially the steamboats were built for carrying cargo and crew only and they were relatively slow and uncomfortable. By 1870 "everyone who was anyone" wanted to travel the Mississippi on a paddle wheel and the great steamboats such as the *Robert E. Lee* and the *Natchez* grew in size—measuring over 300 feet long and weighing over 1,500 tons. They could make the trip from New Orleans to St. Louis in less than four days. It was in such a boat that my daughter, my grandchildren, and I traveled on the second leg of our trip southeast to bury my son-in-law Harry in Charleston in 1867.

Because of the booming fur trade, St. Louis continued to grow and prosper. At the height of the Great Plains fur trade (1815 to 1830) a single Indian agent reported selling 25,000 beaver pelts per year, which totaled over 375,000 beavers over the entire period. One historian stated that, in that same period, $3,750,000.00 worth of beaver pelts passed through St Louis. By 1820 great limestone houses had been erected in the town, and it supported three newspapers and a bookstore. The waterfront was lined with taverns and grog shops where trappers, traders, river men, wagoneers, ex-soldiers, and drifters gambled, drank, boasted and fought. There were also many duels fought between gentlemen in the period between 1820 and 1840. In 1822 St. Louis was incorporated into a city. Eventually, the demand for beaver decreased because the gentlemen of Europe began to prefer silk hats to felt. The price of a beaver pelt had dropped from five dollars in 1829 to just 85 cents in 1846 on the London market. This drop in price was bad for the trapper and trader but good for the beaver. Had the 60 years of over-trapping of the beaver continued for ten more years they probably would have ceased to exist as a species. However, St. Louis was already well established by that time as the "Gateway to the West". Outfitters sold everything that anyone would need (and many things they would not need) to travel west, whether it be by boat, wagon, horseback, or hiking. By 1840 St. Louis had obtained a population of 16,000.

It is not the first time that one of the most important trade and travel centers in the United States was built at the junction of the Mississippi and Missouri Rivers. Between 850 and 1150 AD the largest city in the history of what would eventually become the United States was built across the river from where St. Louis is today. This Native American city was called Cahokia and it had a population of about 10,000 people. Its population was not surpassed until Philadelphia grew to over 10,000 in 1800. The city's inhabitants were temple mound builders and they spread their influences as far away as Florida and Texas. Their purification rites included the use of a powerful emetic know as the Black Drink. Cahokia ceased to exist as a city at the end of the fifteenth century but it continued to influence other cultures into the eighteenth century.

Chapter Three

An Unhappy Existence

After my mother died of a white man's disease, my white stepmother brought me up. My brother was raised in the wilderness. Because my father was frequently gone on business, my living in his home was a rather awkward arrangement, as you can imagine. I was accepted, as a half-breed slave, into my father's fine, aristocratic, white household by my stepmother and my two stepsisters. Since my father had a dark Spanish complexion, the fact that I was half Indian was not readily apparent to the citizens of St. Louis excepting the members of my immediate family. Therefore, I was permitted to attend school along with my stepsisters.

Although I was treated like a slave at home, life in general was tolerable until the death of my father in 1820. He was fatally wounded, presumably by a whore, while attending a health spa in one of the more affluent districts of St. Louis. To avoid scandal, his death certificate stated, "Died of natural causes". I alone was at his side when he died because I happened to be cleaning rooms in the spa at the time he was wounded. I was only eleven years old at the time and suddenly felt alone in the world and at a loss for how I would be able to survive without my father to protect me. I feared that the cruel way my stepmother and stepsisters treated me in private would become worse and they might throw me out, sell me as a slave, or even have me killed. I was in utter despair until my father called me to his side and, with his last breath, told me a secret that would give me a reason to live and allow me to endure any hardship that my cruel adopted family or the world in general could exact on me. The secret my father told me also provided me with a clue to how he was killed and why, and I vowed to avenge his death when the opportunity presented itself.

My father's wake and the subsequent burial was a major event in St. Louis because my stepmother came from a prominent family and my father had amassed a great deal of wealth via his fur trapping business and other activities both scrupulous and unscrupulous. My Father left no will and very few written records of his business activities and, certainly, no written records of his travels into the American frontier. The only physical evidence of his travels was the forts he had caused to be built and the children he had fathered.

Naturally, my father's white wife and my white stepsisters claimed all of his possessions including the house in which we lived. I received nothing and was promptly severed from the lineage that might someday allow me to inherit. I was no longer allowed to go to school and, without my father's protection and support, was not only a slave within my stepmother's household but was also required to work at several jobs outside the home and to give the money to my stepmother to pay for my keep. Such was my lot in life, and life would have been unbearable if

I had not had the secret and one actual physical possession that my father passed on to me.

Although I could not use the secret or the other possession, nor did I fully recognize their significance, just having them with me was enough to sustain me until I could leave St. Louis behind and follow the trail west—perhaps finding my brother or some of my mother's people and learning their ways. This opportunity presented itself when I was thirteen years old in the form of an advertisement placed by William Ashley in the *Missouri Gazette and Advertiser.*

Chapter Four

Into the Wilderness

William Ashley knew of my late father's fur business and wanted to follow in his footsteps. It was not necessary to worry about my father as competition because he did not pass the company on. His fur business died with him. Ashley's advertisement asked for "enterprising young men" who would be willing to go into the wilderness. I was, of course, not a young man but I was very tall for my age—extremely tall for a young woman. I had not yet begun to fill out, so I could easily pass for a young man between the ages of 14 and 16 as long as nobody looked too closely. My plan was to make sure they did not get the chance to look too close by keeping to myself as much as possible.

I hired on as a horse wrangler, one of the jobs I had worked at on and off for the last year or so. Not many of the men who were hired had experience in mountain life, although several of them would become famous mountain men in the future—capturing the imagination of would-be frontiersmen. My future traveling companions included Jed Smith, Jim Bridger, Tom Fitzpatrick, Hugh Glass, the Sublette brothers, James Clyman, and Edward

Rose. Most members of our party were respectable enough and would eventually gain the admiration of their employer, their colleagues, and historians, with the possible exception of Edward Rose. Mr. Rose was a large man. He was half Cherokee and half Negro and he had been a Mississippi riverboat pirate and bandit. He soon became my closest friend—my confidant and my protector. Mr. Rose had his reasons for befriending me, but I did not become aware of this until much later.

The largest part of our group did not begin their travels up the Missouri to trap beaver until the spring of 1823, but I was itching to go west so I went with Andrew Henry and some of the others to help build a fort near the mouth of the Yellowstone River in the spring of 1822. I had also been employed as the helper of a general handyman prior to the trip so I was already quite proficient with hammer and nail.

In the spring of 1823 the rest of our trapping party arrived in what was to become the Dakota Territory and we were attacked by Anikara Indians. This being our first confrontation with hostile Indians, we had no idea what to expect nor did we have any idea why we were being attacked. We would all certainly have been killed had not a group of Sioux warriors rallied to our side. We found out later that the Sioux were simply returning a favor since a group of white traders had helped the Sioux defend themselves against an attack by the Anikara the previous year. The trappers had apparently killed three Anikaras in that confrontation and that is the reason they had just attacked us.

The Sioux are the long time inhabitants of the area between the Black Hills and the Bighorn Mountains. We were in their territory and they certainly treated us like welcome guests. I felt a special kinship towards them. We, as a group, and others who came to the area after us, were so impressed with the Sioux lifestyle, their honesty, and their customs that most mountain men eventually took it as a complement when they were told that they looked and acted like Indians.

The mountain men were a hardy lot and, because of their shaggy hair, ruddy complexions, and buckskin clothing, were usually hard to distinguish from the Indians they admired. They fought with and lived among the Indians—sometimes killed them, and sometimes married them. I was, of course, actually a mountain woman but after a year in the wilderness I began to look, act, and even smell like a mountain man myself. I learned to trap the beaver for our fur company and learned to trap and kill nearly every other kind of animal for food, skins, and other uses. We eventually learned from the Indians that virtually every part of an animal could be used for some purpose. It was just a matter of experience. We frequently watched and helped the Indians prepare their animals because they had been doing it for thousands of years. The techniques they used were passed on to them by their ancestors and they were more than willing to pass on these skills to us.

As I said before, we learned a lot about the ways of the wilderness from the Indians, but the main reason why most of us had come into the western wilderness was to acquire beaver pelts. We were not traders like those who had come before us however, we were trappers. We learned how to trap the beaver from the Indian, but beaver trapping was hard work; it was time consuming; and it took patience. Beaver hunters had to dig around the beaver lodges (some of us called them dams) and lay a net around the area to keep the beaver from escaping.

Sometimes they even crashed through the top of the lodge and stabbed the beaver with a spear. The beavers were very cunning animals however, and often eluded capture by even the most practiced hunter. It has been said that most English would-be beaver trappers seldom killed any beaver because they were not patient enough to lay a long siege, and they were often deceived by the beavers' cunning evasions.

By the early 1820's when I started trapping beaver we had a great advantage over our predecessors. We had steel traps. Each one of us, when we were able to acquire enough of them, would carry between six and twelve of these traps at any one time. We would set these traps in shallow water along the edges of streams and rivers. Above the traps we would place a willow branch with its end exposed. This willow tip would be dipped in beaver scent and the twig would be jabbed in the bank of the stream. The trap would be attached to a chain that was anchored in deep water. When the beaver swam up to investigate the scent on the tip of the stick, it would put its foot in the trap. When this happened the beaver would instinctively swim for deep water. The weight of the heavy steel trap and chain would very quickly drag the beaver down under the water and it would drown.

Effectively, the steel trap revolutionized the beaver trapping business. Trapping the beaver became much less time consuming and I or any of my fellow trappers could work alone rather than having to depend on others to help. We could also do other things while we were waiting on the beaver to take the bait and fill our trap. There was a lot of friendly competition between company trappers and free trappers alike to see how many pelts each could acquire in a single season. It was common for a well experienced and adequately equipped white trapper to bring in three to four hundred pelts in a year's time. Some did better. As far as I am aware, Jed Smith holds the all-time yearly trapping record. In what has been called his "big year" in 1825, he single-handedly brought in 668 pelts. Although I became very adept at beaver trapping and brought in my share, I never approached that mark.

Once the beaver was caught, it had to be skinned and stretched over a willow frame to dry. This was time consuming, messy, and tedious work. As I may have mentioned before, some of the men employed Indian squaws to do this work and other less desirable work around the mountain man camp. I, of course, did all this work myself.

As I previously stated, I left St. Louis with several secrets and one possession. My main method of guarding against the discovery of these secrets and safe guarding this possession was to have no close contact with my traveling companions and never to talk to them. This was not always possible and two of my secrets would certainly have soon been revealed had it not been for my growing friendship with Mr. Rose. He had apparently been aware from the beginning that I was a young woman and that I was the half-breed daughter of the late Manuel Lisa. After he had told me that he knew these things about me he was somehow able to stay close to me at all times and helped me guard my secrets from everyone else, including the Indians. Since he appeared not to be the sort of man to molest a young woman, and his size and skill with all types of weapons deterred anyone else from getting closer to me than was wanted, this arrangement of ours seemed to be a good one. He never asked me to reveal any other secrets about my self and he offered nothing concerning his own past to me other than he was also a half-breed of sorts himself.

After two years in the mountains trapping beaver and learning the ways of the wilderness from the Indians, Mr. Ashley decided that it was time to explore further to the west and hopefully find fresh areas where the beaver were more plentiful. One of the Sioux braves had told him that he knew of a notch in the Rocky Mountain range that would allow us to pass through to the western side of these mountains. "Swashbuckling" Tom Fitzgerald volunteered to lead the party, and Mr. Rose, I, and several others opted to accompany him. The young brave who, for some reason, seemed very familiar to me, led us through the notch in the mountain wall and over to the other side.

As Mr. Ashley had hoped, we came upon virgin trapping grounds with a startling abundance of beaver and a myriad of other game of known and unknown species. This was a great find because the demand for beaver hats was great in European cities like London and American cities such as New York. I already knew these facts since I had overheard my father talking about the details of his fur trade dynasty when he was at our home in St. Louis. However, we were not aware of the fact that other kinds of pelts were wanted as well, such as marten, fox, and otter to decorate items of clothing and to make the clothing warmer. These critters, excepting the otter, were also in abundance, and our Indian guide was very instrumental in helping us learn the skills we needed to catch them.

The area around this notch in the mountain wall later became know as South Pass and would become part of a major route for white settlers moving from east to west on the Oregon Trail. There were two trapping seasons—one in the fall and one in the spring. We had to find a sheltered place to hole up in the winter and a place to rest and rejuvenate in the summer. The winter was a hard time because we still had to find food to survive as well as try to stay warm, plus there was a lot to do to prepare the pelts we had gathered for shipment and sale.

As I have said, many of the trappers employed Indian girls to do some of the more distasteful tasks and also to keep them warm and entertained during the long winter nights. During the summer life was much better. It became common practice to re-supply trapping parties and to give the trappers their yearly pay during the lazy days of summer. The anticipation of their yearly pay and the hopes of getting something other than fatty meat to eat and something other than mountain water to drink also kept the mountain men and their concubines from straying from their trapping parties and striking off on their own as independents.

The area around South Pass came to be called Henry's Fork and it became a common practice for trapping parties, freelance trappers and Indians to sell their wares there and barter for other items. In the summer of 1825 this gathering of trappers, Indians, and outfitters became know as a rendezvous. The first rendezvous I am aware of was at Henry's Fork in 1825 and it was a big event lasting a full month. All manner of foodstuffs, essential survival items such as powder and ball, such convenience items as could be utilized in the wilderness, alcohol, and even women were bought and sold at the rendezvous that year and yearly rendezvous in various places thereafter. The alcohol of choice was Taos Lightning and the woman of choice seemed to be the young squaw just out of puberty. The standard price for a squaw was a good jug of whisky or a good horse. A chief's most beautiful daughter was usually worth two good horses. Although I was much less comely than a chief's prettiest daughter and my protector Mr. Rose was ever—present and watchful, I kept my face and body well covered during these rambunctious events.

Apart from previously mentioned yearly celebrations the life of a fur trapper was hard, tedious, lonely and dangerous but it was also very profitable. During the mountain man's heyday a carpenter or a mason commonly received one dollar and fifty cents a day for his labors. Beaver pelts sold for two to four dollars a pound at the rendezvous and six to eight dollars a pound in St. Louis. The individuals who bought the pelts from the trappers and resold them in St. Louis and resupplied the trappers during the annual rendezvous were in an even more lucrative business than the trappers. They not only made 300 percent profit on the sale of the pelts, but they shamelessly marked up all the goods they sold to the trappers. Probably the biggest mark up was on whiskey, which, of course, all the mountain men demanded. In St. Louis whiskey sold for thirty cents a gallon. The re-suppliers cut it with water and sold it to the trappers at the annual rendezvous for three dollars a pint.

After the 1826 rendezvous Mr. Ashley, our boss and re-supplier, retired and sold his fur business to Jed Smith, Edward Rose, and me. By this time it had become increasingly difficult to hide my identity because, in spite of my manly labors and my meager diet, I was developing into a full-bodied woman with large but firm breasts and rounding hips. Since I was nearly six feet tall I would have been quite a sight to behold while bathing in a stream or lake, and my colleagues would have had quite a shock if they had espied me devoid of my leather garments. As far as I am aware, the members of my trapping party never observed this open display of my womanly charms. This is partly due to the fact (it now disgusts me to recall) that these instances of naked bathing were few and far between and, to be sure, I was very cautious—making sure that detection would be difficult. The fact that I had no facial hair would have been easier to explain if I had wanted to reveal that I was part Indian, but this fact I also wanted to conceal as long as possible. I was very grateful that Jed Smith chose to remain clean-shaven even though the absence of a beard was quite uncharacteristic of the mountain man. Of course my faithful protector also played along and shaved when he could although it was difficult for him because he was inflicted with a condition common to the Negro that causes bumps on the skin due to ingrown facial hair. A bout with the straight razor or razor-sharp hunting knife could turn into a painful, tedious, and often bloody experience. Often times Mr. Rose was not up to the task. Because it was in my own best interest that Mr. Smith and Mr. Rose remain clean-shaven, I became their personal barber. For the next four years we traveled, trapped, traded, and explored the greater part of the Louisiana Territory as well as the Oregon territory. I espied with my own eyes such sites as the Pacific Ocean, where we learned to trap sea otter, the giant redwoods, and even Colter's Hell. We, of course, attended all the rendezvous and even made a trip or two to the arid northern plains. The Great Plains were too dry and barren to yield any significant number of pelts, but I was drawn to this area by what my father had whispered to me on his deathbed nearly ten years before. However, at the same time, I did not linger there very long because I was determined to safeguard my secret from the other members of my party at all costs. My dying father had told me, "Trust no one".

Eventually we all, me especially, grew tired of the life of the fur trapper and trader. Anyway, of the 33 trappers and adventurers that followed Jed Smith over the last few years, only seven were still around to tell the tale, and only five of us returned with him. I, being one of these, vowed to find a less dangerous occupation for myself should I actually return to the next rendezvous alive. I had been frost bit, snake bit, stabbed with a knife and a spear, shot, mauled by a grizzly bear and several Indians and a few white men as well. Apart from that, on more than one occasion I nearly died of starvation, dehydration, hypothermia, and exhaustion. Since we all had enough money for a stake, we sold our fur company, later to be called The Rocky Mountain Fur Company, to Tom Fitzpatrick, Jim Bridger, and three other men.

Chapter Five

My Coming Out

Wanting to eventually gravitate north, I invested my stake in a small trading post at the Popo Agie River near the southern end of the Bighorn River. This had been the sight of the 1829 mountain man Rendezvous and it was scheduled to be the site for the 1830 Rendezvous as well. One of the first items I purchased, in addition to the trading post, was a store-bought dress after the fashion of those I had seen worn by high-society Spanish women in California. I was 21 now and if I was going to come out and be a woman, I was going to do it in style.

Naturally my faithful longtime companion Mr. Rose, who obviously survived our adventures with Jed Smith as well, volunteered to help me at the trading post. I was starting to become wary of Mr. Rose's intentions toward me, especially after the first time I put on that dress. Later on, it would become evident that he also had had another reason for sticking close to me for all these years. I was not able to dwell on Mr. Rose's intentions much though because I was too busy preparing for the 1830 rendezvous, and I was excited. I was excited for two reasons. First, it was the first time I would be a buyer of pelts rather than a seller, and a seller of supplies and other things the trappers would want instead of a buyer of these things. Second, it was the first time I would be present at a rendezvous dressed as a woman.

I had observed, first hand, all the things that went on in the month of rendezvous—the drinking, the gambling, the fighting, the duels, the rodeo type competitions, the shooting competitions, the knife throwing contests, the fun and games, the dancing and even the fornication. All this was done quite openly. It was common for a trapper to spend and/or lose his entire yearly pay at a rendezvous. It seemed that some of the trappers even wanted it that way. They were willing to work hard, risking their lives every day for eleven months, so they could blow the entire amount, which in the 1820's was usually between $1,000.00 and $2,000.00, in one month of continuous, blissful chaos.

As I said, I had observed this chaos but I had never been an active participant in it. So, in the summer of 1830 on the first night of the Popo Agie River Rendezvous, I soaked the grime off my body in the large wooden tub I had caused to be built so I could provide hot baths to the mountain men when they came to the rendezvous. I even added a little jasmine—scented bath oil. Then, I put on my store-bought dress and joined in the festivities.

Mr. Rose accompanied me to the festivities, but he had been drinking, which I had never seen him do before, and he had a strange grin on his face, which made me feel uncomfortable. He insisted that we walk arm in arm just like he was a proper escort accompanying a proper lady to a dance. This was a new experience for me, playing the role of a woman in close contact with a man, and my escort must have mistaken my nervous shudders for something else because he drew me to him and started to run his hands roughly over my body. When I tried to resist his amorous overtures he tore my dress and forced me to the muddy ground. I was a tall woman and strong and I had always been able to defend myself against men and beasts alike but tonight it was different. My movement was encumbered by the dress and Mr. Rose seemed to be possessed of superhuman strength. I had never fought with him before, but I had not anticipated that he could completely overpower me; even though he was slightly taller than I and must have out—weighed me by at least 50 pounds. He had a death grip on me that I could not break, and he had me pinned to the ground. I could feel my consciousness slipping away as he pried apart my legs and prepared to rape me on the cool wet ground. Suddenly I heard the sickly thud of metal on bone and I was released. I pushed the unconscious body of my once trusted companion off me and stared up into the wild but sympathetic eyes of the largest man I had ever seen. There was no doubt that he was my rescuer because he stood over me with a pistol in his hand which he held by the barrel, and even in the dim light, I could see blood and fragments of skin on the butt.

My knight in shining armor, actually greasy buckskin, was a French-Canadian mountain man of Métis' descent. He was a huge man of huge proportions. He had large hands and feet and, as I would soon find out, even larger appetites. I also found out later that he had a huge ego and a huge temper. He would, in fact, eventually be known as "the Bully of the Mountains". However, the characteristic that would most accurately define him in later years was a huge thirst and a huge capacity for

Taos Lightning. At the moment though, he was my hero and I probably owed my life to him. Regaining my senses with great effort, I struggled to my feet and looked down at the now hideous form of the man who had befriended me, protected me and accompanied me through seven years of hardship, exciting adventures, and astounding discoveries. I found I loved him, despised him, pitied him, and was drawn to him and repulsed by him at the same time. I wanted to hug him, revive him, and dress his wound but I also wanted to put a bullet through his head to make sure he was dead. I fell to my knees and I cried for the man on the ground in front of me. I wailed, I screamed, I blubbered, I cursed, and I kicked at him and spat at him. I even sprang upon him and assailed him with my fists.

I had forgotten about the man who had stood next to me with the characteristic "stupid look" upon his face until he grabbed me up in his huge paws and shook me until my teeth rattled and my eyes nearly separated from their sockets. The display that I put on must have been more than the big man could take. In any case, that thorough shaking set me right, and when my head was clear, I took the giant's arm and allowed him to lead me away from what I believed to be the corpse of my ex-friend Mr. Rose. We left him for dead and I remember thinking as we left him on the damp ground in the rain, "He does not deserve to be buried". For better or worse, when I later passed by the spot were Mr. Rose had fallen, his body was no longer there, and as I found out later he still lived, was in good hands, and had a few secrets of his own.

Joseph Chouinard my future husband and soon to be my first lover and the father of my children, was born in 1798 in Canada and had been a fur trapper and mountain man since he was a teenager. He was Métis but had reportedly been married to a French woman in Québec in 1818, although he had never talked about it and I had never seen any evidence of it. I had never seen him nor even heard of him prior to the 1830 rendezvous but he was as charming as he was noble that first night, so much so that I invited him back to my cabin, which was also my trading post, to clean up.

I had left the water in my large wooden tub and the water was still warm. So I stripped off my clothes and got in the tub, leaving Joseph inside the cabin. This was, perhaps, not a prudent thing to do but I just did not care anymore. I had been nearly raped and killed less than an hour before and I had survived more than seven years in the wilderness always hiding my womanliness and never experiencing the kind of love that could be shared between a man and a woman. It was time—my time to be loved.

After a while Joseph came out of my cabin with a half empty jug of full strength Taos Lightning partially concealed in one of his huge hands. He espied me outside in the light of the July moon sitting in my wooden tub. I gestured that there was room for one more and he was naked and in the tub beside me post haste. Joseph offered me the jug and I took it from him. I had tasted whiskey before, but I had had more on me than in me in the last seven years. Whiskey was commonly used externally as a disinfectant and internally as a pain killer by those who lived in the wilderness. We fur trappers felt it was too expensive to be guzzled just to get drunk.

I took a couple of good pulls from the bottle of Taos Lightning and handed it back to Joseph who took a few good pulls and handed it back to me. We subsequently handed the bottle back and forth several times and the rest of the night was a blur as we alternated between intense activity and dosing until I woke up in my bed way past dawn, still naked but alone. I had no idea how I had gotten there nor did I know where Joseph was. The only shreds of physical proof I had that our night of lovemaking, which haunted my memory, really happened at all were my nakedness and the aching in my loins. Oh yes—he had been there. And the whiskey had been there as well.

Once I was fully awake I tried to stand but a wave of nausea hit me and I fell dizzily back onto the bed. I had purged my stomach several times and my head throbbed and felt as heavy as a large melon. Later I got the dry heaves and I thought my back would break but there was no relief from my body's attempt to rid itself of the poison I had put into it the night before. Finally, I slept. When I awoke it was dark again and, although my head still pounded, I was able to get up, dress and go outside. The festivities of the rendezvous were just starting up again and most of the mountain men, the Indians, and the traders I knew by sight were present. Only Joseph (I did not even know his last name at the time) and Edward Rose were missing. I could never have guessed at that moment, that I would see neither Joseph Chouinard nor Edward Rose again for more than five years.

By the end of the rendezvous I was utterly distraught, I thought sure that Joseph would come back to be with me again if he could, and I began thinking that Mr. Rose must have found him and took his revenge. I was also worried that Mr. Rose would come back and finish the business he started with me or even kill me. I had always been a courageous young woman but after a month went by I began to feel like something had changed within me—that I had something to protect. It was like there was more than just me to be responsible for and the feeling scared me.

I soon found out why I had these strange feelings of anxiety. My first lover—my large, hard drinking, hard loving, chivalrous Frenchman, absent now for several weeks, had left me with something of himself. He had left me with child. If my mountaineering existence had ill prepared me for the physical expression of love, it had certainly not prepared me to be a mother. Luckily, I was born with some unlearned instincts on how to cope with my situation. Ordinarily I would have probably been able to give birth on my own, like the Indians of the plains and the mountains had done for centuries, but nothing could have adequately prepared me for the ordeal of giving birth to twins with a combined weight of over 15 pounds. Where was my midwife, where were my trusty companions of the mountains, where was the father of these two faceless, nameless torturers writhing inside me? The Rendezvous was over. There was not another living soul, save a handful of wandering Indians, within 50 miles. Most of my fellow adventurers were dead, and my oldest and closest friend and probably the father of these soon-to-be-born children, as far as I knew then, were also dead.

Chapter Six

Bringing Twins Into the World

When their time came, my twin boy and girl ripped and tore their way out into the world. I was powerless to stop them or to help them. During the several hours that it took for them to free themselves from my womb I wished for death a thousand times. Finally it was over, and the next thing I knew I was tying off their cords and slicing them free from the afterbirths with my skinning knife. Luckily, I had seen this done by a squaw a few years before. Even though I was worn and torn from giving birth to my yet nameless children, I had not the luxury of lying around in bed recuperating. I had to feed myself, fashion some clothes for my new charges, and make something with which to carry them around on my back. I dared not leave them alone in the wild to fall prey to all manner of carnivorous animal or even hostile Indians or marauding white men. I was able to make a rude rucksack with two compartments out of young willow branches and some old hides. It was hard work packing my fast growing children around on my back, but I was a strong young woman and I was also accustomed to carrying a heavy pack, a rifle, and other gear through the mountains.

Happily, I only had to carry my children for short distances. I had already decided however, that as soon as it was feasible, I would take my babies and what necessities we could carry and head further north.

Chapter Seven

The Call of the Canyon

As my children grew stronger and began to walk I started planning for our trip and foraging for all manner of lightweight foodstuffs that we could take along. I had learned from the Indians and the mountain men how to cut and dry meat, which berries, roots, and plants were fit to eat, and I had learned what herbs could be used to season food, to aid in curing illnesses and to help heal wounds. I gathered all these things and my children, now known as Joseph and Maria, happily helped me. I called them my children not our children because after nearly three years, I had lost all hope of ever seeing their father again. It was easier for me to face the fact that he was dead rather than imagine that he had willingly deserted me. We had gathered what was needed for the trip; my children were ready; and I was ready. Our final destination was near. I had the map—the one possession my father passed on to me and I remembered the last words of the secret that he whispered to me on his deathbed. "Follow the map. Go to the canyon. You will find it there. Trust no one."

We headed straight north following the Bighorn River and then east toward the Bighorn Mountains. It was hard going and we had to rest often. I traveled in constant fear of meeting even a single hostile Indian because I was not confident that I could defend my children and myself at the same time. They were, of course, too young to defend themselves but they were good little travelers and never complained. They had known, in their short lives, only hardship and had grown accustomed to our lonely existence. No, they had not really grown accustomed to it. They knew nothing else. So, they were innocents alone in the world excepting the companionship of their brother or sister, and me. My children knew no childhood games, because I knew no such games to teach them. They had no children's toys because I had never seen a children's toy so I had no example to use to fashion one for them had I deemed it necessary.

As we left the river and approached the mountains, the country became increasingly barren and dry. It was hard to find water and game. We were forced to subsist on the dried meat, roots and berries that we still carried, and the meat was nearly gone. Soon we would be entering the mountains and, although it was early summer, there was still snow on the peaks and, possibly, even on the pass I sought. It would be critical to enter the mountains at the right place in order to find the pass as soon as possible, and I had only a very slight remembrance of where that point of entrance might be located. I had been there before but not without a guide. Now it was my turn to be the guide and I was hoping I was up to it. I was thinking that I might be able to survive on my own in the wilderness almost indefinitely, but it was only a matter of time before we would be confronted by the wrong tribe of Indians and my children would most certainly be in danger.

There was that anxious feeling again which I knew now was a mother's natural instinct to protect her young and her fear for their well-being. I felt this feeling because I knew there was no love lost between me and most of the tribes that roamed through these mountains which we must cross, and they would certainly show neither my children nor me any mercy. I had no doubts that they would kill me slowly, and the best I could hope for would be that my children would be killed quickly. Any alternative to this scenario was unthinkable.

Chapter Eight

The Mission from Washington

At the time we were preparing to enter the mountains from the west, when I was contemplating all the dangers that could confront me and my children, I was not aware that the gravest threat to my children and me and the fulfillment of my ultimate quest was one white man by the name of Benjamin Bonneville, who was just entering these same mountains from the eastern side. I was soon to find out why he was there. The official story was that Captain Bonneville of the United States Army had applied for and received a two-year leave of absence from the army in order to become a fur trader. His leave of absence was pushed through army channels very rapidly and he had also received a large sum of money from an unknown eastern source which was to be used to finance his fur trading ventures.

So, Mr. Bonneville, with no experience in the fur trade and at a time when the fur trade was beginning to wane, set out for the west. When he arrived there he headed north and, in 1832, caused a fort to be built on the Green River near South Pass in a place that would later become southwest Wyoming. The fort was in the middle of Blackfoot country and when Captain

Bonneville abandoned it in early 1833, shortly after it was completed, the Indians raided it and burnt it to the ground. The site of the Bonneville's fort was, however the same sight used for the 1833 rendezvous.

Historians have suggested that Captain Bonneville was never on a leave of absence from the United States Army and that he was sent out west to gather military intelligence in the British controlled Oregon Territory and in California, which was under Spanish rule at the time. This may be partly true but the fact is Captain Bonneville never ventured into the British or the Spanish domains. He sent a smart, handsome, tall riding mountain man by the name of Joseph Walker to do that for him. By the time that Mr. Walker had returned to Green River for the 1833 Rendezvous Captain Bonneville had already ridden through South Pass and was heading northeast in order to enter the Bighorn Mountains from the east. I was soon to find out that the Army had provided Captain Bonneville with a double cover. He came out west because he knew part of my secret and he had to find me to either find out the rest or confirm that the secret had died with my father.

Prior to my father's death there were a handful of powerful men who knew what my father had been involved in prior to becoming a fur trader, and they had sent agents to New Orleans who then tracked him to St. Louis. They did not know his entire secret but they had heard that he had made a map of some kind and they knew the general area where the map was supposed to lead. After these agents had my father killed in 1820 his room was searched thoroughly but nothing was found other than a small amount of money and such things as a businessman would bring to a spa for a weekend of relaxation. The agents questioned everyone who had any dealings with the spa and found nothing, so the investigation was put on hold. However, a few years later, they found out through an informant that one of the young girls who had regularly worked at the spa had disappeared. Later they heard rumors that this little girl had been seen leaving Manuel Lisa's room shortly after their paid assassin had left him for dead.

The wilderness of the west is a large area and, although the agents searched for that little girl for years after they had heard that she might have gone west with Mr. Ashley, she was not found. The fact that she had not been found was also partly because the members of Ashley's party were not aware that they had a young woman with them and also due to the fact that nearly all of Ashley's original party were already dead by the time the agents decided to pursue this lead. In 1830 my pursuers from Washington received a new lead. Someone who had attended the 1830 Rendezvous had seen a woman of about the right age, after the first day of the Rendezvous, asking after a huge Frenchman. Captain Bonneville was dispatched to the west to find this mysterious woman but had thought her location to be near the Green River rather than the Popo Agie River. Ascertaining that the young woman must have ventured off somewhere, he built his fort and waited for her return. By the time he realized his mistake and started toward where he thought she should be going, she (I) had already departed by another route. However, our paths were soon to cross.

Finally, I found the entry point into the mountains that I was looking for. However, before we started our ascent into the Bighorn Mountains we stopped at a small trading post that would later become the small Wyoming town of Tensleep. We were hot, tired, thirsty, and nearly starved after traveling some one hundred and forty miles, mainly on foot, through the arid valley between the Absaroka Range and the Bighorn Mountains. In addition, my two old mules needed rest, water, and proper fodder. We had another need for stopping as well. We were in Blackfoot country and these were one of the few tribes of Indians my father had not succeeded in befriending.

I knew sign and I could speak a few words of the Blackfoot language, but with them parley would not be an option. I needed reinforcements if we were going to make it through the some 60 miles of mountainous terrain and reach our final destination—the canyon shown on the map. I had not yet seen the canyon that held the secret that, unbeknown to me at the time, powerful men in the east would be more than willing to kill me to protect. Had I know the extent of the danger that awaited us in those beautiful green mountains I should have given up my quest and stayed with my small charges in Tensleep or turned back and returned to the mouth of the Bighorn River.

In Tensleep I was able to recruit a handful of renegade Sioux who I outfitted to accompany us through the mountains. However, they had no horses and there were no horses to be had. So, my two children and I accompanied by four old Indians and two old mules and carrying what ammunition and food that was available for purchase at the trading post, set out on our trek across the Bighorns from west to east.

Upon leaving the trading post we entered a beautiful green river valley with picturesque grey cliffs guarding it on the southern side and fields of multicolored wildflowers decorating the riverbank. The weather was fine and, although it was slow going because one mule was loaded with supplies and my two children were tied to the top of the other mule, I did not mind the walk. The children soon asked to be untied so that they could walk as well and they began to frolic in the meadow— picking wildflowers and learning the Lakota names for each flower from the gentle-natured Indians who accompanied us. This was a wonderful sight. I could almost imagine, seeing the six of them together and enjoying each other as they were, that my Joseph and Marie had found their long-lost grandfathers and uncles.

As we continued along toward our destination, the path became increasingly steeper and sometimes it seemed that it led to nowhere except to a wall of solid rock, but then we would find a crevice in that rock and, with little difficulty, find our way through to the other side. Eventually the country opened up and we found ourselves in a vast mountain valley abounding with pine, aspen, and birch trees and several kinds of berry bushes. We saw several deer and elk and even a few bears, as well as many types of varmints and birds. In these beautiful surroundings we decided to stop and camp for the night after traveling about 20 miles.

When darkness came the old tensions and anxiety returned and I became watchful. It was nothing to me to rely on only two hours of sleep each night and, even then, I often slept with one eye open. This was a standard practice born of necessity when living in the wilderness. Some sort of potential danger was always lurking just beyond the shadows. I had been schooled well—since I had spent the last 10 years in the wild.

Our first evening in the mountains passed without incident. We awoke at dawn and, after a quick meal of freshly caught brook trout, pan baked biscuits and camp style coffee, we continued up the trail. We followed this trail along a stream for many hours and began to hear the songs of the meadowlarks, which were in abundance in that area. Then, we saw the lake. It was a large lake. The water was clear and, even in the height of summer, very cold. This however, did not deter my young offspring from taking to it like waterfowl. I let them have their afternoon on the banks of the lake. They alternatively dog paddled in the lake and sunned themselves on the sandy shore.

All too soon night had fallen and the air turned cool. We found shelter in an old trapper's cabin and utilized it in the way of the mountain man. It was customary in those days to leave your cabin stocked with all manner of food and other supplies, according to the needs of the area and your ability to provide these necessities, and leave the door unlocked so that other travelers could use the cabin for shelter as long as necessary. It was also customary for the traveler to restock the cabin if he had the means or to return to the cabin at some later date and restock it then. We had just re-supplied ourselves two days before so I was able to restock the cabin with some of the niceties that were uncommon in the mountains such as real bacon grease, not bear fat, some corn meal, and real coffee.

When the Indians had made themselves comfortable outside the cabin next to their fire and my children were fast asleep in our small bed, I lay awake and reflected on the day. We had only traveled 10 miles. I also contemplated what the next few days of traveling would be like and what dangers lay ahead. Even though we had had a good meal and we were sheltered from the elements by that well built cabin, danger seemed close at hand. What kind of danger it was I could not perceive.

The next morning when my small family and I filed out of the cabin the fire was cold and our four Indian companions were gone. I dared not track them because I had my children to protect. So, we had a quick breakfast and prepared to make a start. That is when I discovered that my mules were gone as well. Luckily we had most of our supplies inside the cabin and our Indians or their capturers did not feel it prudent to come in the cabin and take our supplies or our scalps. Since I could do nothing else, I gathered up what supplies I could carry on my back and, with two 28-month-old children in tow, continued up and east toward the Powder River Pass. It was hard going but we were able to travel the five-mile distance in just a couple of hours.

After I had made a meal, we scouted around a little—enjoying the view. The air way cool up there at 9,600 feet above sea level and there was a thick glacier like snow drift just below the pass in an area where the midsummer sun did not often reach. I allowed the children to play in the snow and we had a nice summer snowball fight. After the fun and frolicking, we stood on the edge of a cliff from which we could see many miles of the beautiful valley below us. That is when Joseph, with his sharp young eyes, spotted the Indians. Marie saw them too but my eyesight had been growing steadily worse since I had been conked on the head by a Blackfoot wielding a wooden club back in 1829, so I could not see them. Instinctively though, I knew they were there. Were they Blackfoot or Sioux? I was thinking, if I could answer that question, I could be fairly certain whether we were going to get out of these mountains alive or if we would be killed or taken captive. We would soon find out.

It would do us no good to take shelter and try to hide. If we had seen the Indians then they had certainly seen us as well.

It was time to fly or fight. Since it was impossible to outrun the Indians on foot accompanied as I was by a couple of two year olds, I decided to do neither. I just packed up our supplies and we continued east over the crest of the pass and down the other side. Within an hour the Indians came whooping down upon us. I was thinking that they certainly would have killed us immediately had they not been so surprised at seeing a woman and two small children alone on the top of a bald mountain in broad daylight. The fact that I never fired a shot even though I was well armed and the fact that we did not try to run also apparently intrigued them.

Once the Indians got close, I realized that they were neither Sioux nor Blackfoot—they were Crow. This confused me because they were more than 100 miles south of their summer hunting grounds. I soon realized, however, that the braves were, in fact, in the mountains to hunt. They were sent there to hunt me and after looking closely at me and my small children and after conferring with each other for a time, one brave grabbed up my two children and another two threw me over a horse and tied my arms and legs together like a sack of potatoes. After I was transported in this manner for several hours we came upon a large grey army tent pitched in a clearing next to a mountain stream. We abruptly halted and I was untied and unceremoniously thrown to the ground. I then noticed that my beloved twins were tied securely to a tree near where the horses were hobbled. I loudly voiced my dissatisfaction of this in my best Crow, but the braves paid me no mind. They just picked me up and threw me into the army tent. I tumbled across the floor and landed next to a pair of army boots that were attached to feet, legs, a pair of shoulders with captain bars attached to them and the face of a man soon to be identified as Captain Benjamin Bonneville.

Captain Bonneville spoke to me in his cultured eastern English. He said, "Don't bother to get up Miss Lisa. Or is it Mrs.?" He then placed one of his highly polished boots on my windpipe and said, "Let me get right to the point young lady. Where is the map?" I tried to shake my head back and forth and managed to spit on his boot before I drifted into unconsciousness.

When I awoke it was dark and I was naked and alone, and I was no longer in the tent. I was tethered to four stakes in the middle of a small clearing with rawhide strips and the drying strips were beginning to get very tight on my wrists and ankles.

As I lay there in the dark with no way to protect myself from human or nonhuman predators, small animals or even insects, I began to reflect on my life so far. What else did I have to do? What else could I do except wait to be torn apart by a large animal, to be slowly eaten by small ones, or to bleed to death once the flesh on my wrists and ankles was severed by the tightening rawhide? I did not even want to think about what had happened to my babies. So, I reflected.

I arrived in this world as an illegitimate half-breed. I scarcely remember my mother. She died when I was six years old. I had a twin brother who I did not really remember but whose face haunted my dreams. I lived for five years in a house with people who despised me but pretended to love me when my father came home for one of his short visits. Then my father gave me a map and told me a secret and he was gone as well. Did he love me? This is hard to know but it does not matter anymore for he is dead. I chose one of the hardest and most dangerous of occupations when I was 13, partly because I wanted to get away from the people who occupied my father's house and partly because I wanted to go where my father's words had sent me. Was it end of the rainbow? Perhaps, but it was all I had that was truly mine—the only thing that tied me to my roots—the whispered words and a piece of birch bark with lines and circles drawn on it.

After spending more than seven years in the wilderness, posing as a man and doing a man's work, I finally became a woman only to be left sore, bruised, pregnant, and alone after only one night of love. Was it love? I think it was, but it did not matter now because my lover must be dead. Even my children were probably dead. Would I ever know for sure? Probably, I would never know because I was now very close to death myself. I was thinking—what day was it? If this is the first night that I have been lying here, and it must be because, if not, I would surely be dead by now, then it is July 31, 1833—my twenty-fourth birthday.

So, there it is, after all I have been through, it comes down to this. I am lying here on the top of a mountain on the snow-covered ground spread-eagled and naked, in the dark, tied securely with no means of escape, waiting to die on my birthday. I was thinking, could not this be a dream? Then I heard the wolves.

I found out later that after Captain Bonneville had crushed my windpipe with his boot enough to render me unconscious he had had his Indians strip and search me. My young children were also stripped and searched and what little baggage we had with us was also searched. Captain Bonneville had not found what he was looking for and he had not bothered to question me because he thought he knew the entire secret and he had, apparently, not contemplated the possibility that I had committed the map to memory. He had left me for dead and he had no further need for my children. So he told the Indians that they could do what they wanted with them. His mission was over and it was time for him to get back to Washington and brief his superiors that the reconnaissance in the British and Spanish colonies was completed but the search for the map was a failure. In fact, he was prepared to say the map probably did not ever exist.

Stone Wall Jackson would not be pleased that his trusted agent, Captain Bonneville, had not found the map but at least he had disposed of the girl. Just when Captain Bonneville was starting to ride off, leaving my children with the Indians to do with as they pleased, five single shot rifles were fired in rapid succession. As a result, the four Crow braves were mortally wounded and the Army Captain sustained an injury, which would delay his return to Washington by nearly two years.

As I lay there on the ground with the wolves approaching, my mind began to wander. I was thinking, what is insanity? Is one really insane when one loses touch with reality—when the edges of the mind become frayed and start to unravel like an old throw rug that one does not take the time to mend but continues to tread upon until it completely unravels and becomes useless? And I was thinking, how does one lose touch with reality and why? Could it be that when a person has experienced a certain amount of adversity in her life and the pain becomes too great for her to rationally cope with and she begins to create an alternate reality for herself where there is less pain, that she is insane?

Then, when the wolves began to get closer and began to circle me, so close that I could hear them sniffing me like dogs, I believe my mind did actually begin to fray around the edges—threatening to come undone. I no longer feared the wolves because I was no longer there. I was in another reality. I was walking in a field of wild flowers with my babies and their father. It was a beautiful day and we were all holding hands and smiling. All my pursuers had stopped searching for me, my quest was over and the future looked bright and rosy.

The wolves could not smell fear on me and this confused them and made them wary. Perhaps I was not just a naked, defenseless, woman tied to the ground with no means of defending herself. Maybe I had a secret. This possibility made them cautious and maybe it even scared them a little. They were hungry but the carnivores did not want to take any unnecessary risks. However, the curiosity became too much for one of the young wolves and he came up and nipped me on the thigh. Then he retreated back into the pack waiting for a reaction—some sort of retaliation. When there was no reaction and the other wolves saw this and smelled the blood, they apparently realized there was no need for further delay and that I was, in fact, easy prey with no means to defend myself.

I felt the sting of the bite—then a second one and then I heard what sounded like five gunshots. The pain of the bites and the noise of the shots brought me back to the real world and I started screaming. I had nothing to lose. What did it matter if more hostile Indians came or Captain Bonneville came back to finish me off, the wolves would surely kill me anyway and that would be a horrible way to die.

Chapter Nine

Out of the Mouths of Wolves

Soon, I heard three more gunshots and they sounded closer. The wolves had disappeared and I could hear the faint but unmistakable sound of hooves on the rocky ground. Horses were approaching. The sound of someone dismounting close by startled me, but then something heavy and soft was thrown over me and all of the sudden my hands and feet were free. Although I was tired and stiff I lashed out with my hands and my feet as hard as possible, being restricted as I was by the heavy hide robe. As I continued to thrash about I heard a voice whisper gently in my ear in the language of the Omaha. "Easy little sister", the voice said. Then the voice said in plain English, "Your children are unharmed and safe. You are all safe now."

Someone gently bound my wounds so I would not lose more blood and I wrapped the buffalo robe tightly around me, for it was cold. The same man asked me if I could ride. It was still dark, but I replied that I could ride as far as necessary. At that moment, I much preferred riding through the mountains in the dark to lying on the cold, hard, ground naked and being torn to bits and eaten by wolves. So, we rode. We rode for hours. We rode all night.

As dawn approached, I could see that we had ridden completely out of the mountains and were on the Great Plains heading southeast. We stopped to rest, eat, and water the horses at a reservoir and I saw my rescuer more clearly. I saw myself in him and I realized that this slim, hard muscled, Indian brave who stood proudly yet humbly before me was my own twin brother, Raymond. I had not seen him or even been aware of his whereabouts since we were six years old—about the time our mother died. I had been taken to live in the city with my stepmother and stepsisters while Raymond had been raised on the plains in an area that would later be called Nebraska—Omaha country—the land of my mother's people.

I wanted to ask my twin brother a thousand questions, but he signed that we needed to keep moving because an advance party, which included my children, was heading to the next camp as well. He also stated that they could be in danger because there were only three braves with them; and a wounded white soldier also in their company needed care and watching.

After we had traveled east for about five more hours, I saw the dust of horses and, sometime later, we caught up with the advance party. As I got up alongside my children I realized that they were tied to the top of my old pack mule and my other mule was being ridden by one of the Indians who had deserted us at the cabin by the lake a couple of nights ago. Whilst I was giving him an angry stare, which was very embarrassing to an Indian because making eye contact was rare in their culture, Raymond told me that the night the Indians had disappeared they had seen the white man, who was now with us, and some

Crows scouting around in the woods near the cabin where the children and I were sleeping. The Sioux had acted as decoys and had led the white man and the Crows away from the cabin, but three were caught and killed by the Crows. The fourth old Indian was able to get away with the two mules but since he was no match for the Crows alone, he hid the mules in a place only he knew. Then he found Raymond and told him about my predicament. Raymond and his war party had attacked and killed the Crows and wounded the white man. Knowing I was close by, Raymond then came and saved me from being a late dinner for the pack of Bighorn Mountain wolves.

My brother, my children, the rest of our party, and I continued to travel southeast for five more days. We had to stop and rest often because Captain Bonneville nearly died several times during the trip and we wished to keep him alive if we could. We knew that if he died word would get out to an army headquarters and soldiers would eventually track us down and retaliate. This, my brother had learned, was their way. He had seen soldiers slaughter an entire Indian village, including women and children, to avenge the death of just one white soldier. It did not seem to disturb the soldiers in the least if they mistakenly attacked the wrong village. To most of the soldiers and most of the white leadership including President Andrew Jackson himself—an Indian was an Indian and the only good Indian was a dead Indian.

When we got to the temporary village of our mother's people, my brother took Captain Bonneville directly to the dwelling of the medicine man. This man was not just a shaman who claimed to ward off evil spirits and summon helpful ones—he actually had a very solid knowledge of how to properly treat wounds and how to prevent and treat infection. He also knew how to prepare medicines and potions from herbs and other substances. It was customary among this tribe to pass these skills on from generation to generation so that the ancient knowledge of homeopathic healing was not lost to future generations.

The European Americans and their so called holy men were in the process of destroying this knowledge, essential to the survival of the Indians of all tribes, in the name of Christianity. Curiously though, most of the missionaries were located in areas of the southwest where there was wealth to be distributed—gold to fill their personal coffers and the coffers of the European religious organizations. Therefore, these zealous missionaries had not yet arrived in large numbers in the remote areas of the Great Plains.

Once my brother had explained to the medicine man that the white man must live rather than be tortured to death, he brought me to his lodge to meet his wife, his twin children, and the rest of his family. Raymond was married to the old chief's daughter and, because he had a reputation as a great warrior, had considerable influence among other members of the village. Raymond's wife was beautiful and very gracious in her way. She kept her head down and her eyes diverted when Raymond and I entered the lodge. In another culture, her behavior could have been taken for rudeness or at least shyness, but, as I previously stated, I knew that it was not usual for Indians to look each other in the eye, so I took no offence. Raymond's wife, Little Feet, was a very fine boned and petite woman and she did, in fact, have very small feet.

A small scouting party had been sent ahead of our arrival by about two days in which time, Little Feet had made me some very useful gifts. She made me an Indian skirt and jacket from soft deer hide and some comfortable moccasins. It is amazing that these new clothes fit perfectly. One or more of the braves who traveled with us those first days must have had great powers of observation and must have observed me very closely in order to provide such a good description of the size of my body and feet. In any case, the clothes were as comfortable as they were practical for wear in this warm arid land. I was, of course, also extremely grateful to have something to wear besides that heavy buffalo robe, especially during the hot summer days. Raymond's twin boy and girl were a few years older than my twins but nevertheless they seemed to immensely enjoy the company of my twins. They also looked a lot alike. Looks at Eagle, Raymond's son, and Fire in Hair, Raymond's daughter, soon gave my children Indian names. Since it is customary for Indian children to be named for certain peculiar physical features they have or certain peculiar things they have done, my children were named this way as well. Joseph became known in the village as Swims like Dog and Maria became Big Feet. Raymond's son Looks at Eagle was observed when he was very young staring at an eagle for several minutes. This seemed odd to his mother and the others who observed him because the Eagle refused to fly away, and it was unusual for a child of three years to sit in one place and stare at anything for so long. Fire in Hair got her name because she had a feature uncharacteristic of the Indian race even though she was one fourth Spanish. She had bright red hair. My son was given the name Swims like Dog because he loved the water and could dog paddle very fast and far for a two year old boy. Maria got the name Big Feet, because, unlike her aunt Small Feet, she had extremely large feet and hands for such a small child. She was obviously going to be tall like her mother and father.

I liked being in the Indian village and getting reacquainted with my brother and getting to know the other members of his family and the other members of his village. It was a simple but very peaceful existence. Everyone seemed to get along well. If there were conflicts between members of the village they were not observable to me.

It took several months for Captain Bonneville to recover from his wounds, during which time the village medicine man and his two wives faithfully fed and carred for him. Since it was mostly my fault that Captain Bonneville was in their village, I took my turn at preparing and administering his medicines although I despised the man. Learning how to prepare concoctions and potions from the natural ingredients to be found on the plains and learning which medicines are to be dispensed for which ailments would become very useful to me in the future.

When Captain Bonneville was able to stand and walk around he was secured by a long leather strap similar to a dog's leash. One of the stronger braves walked around with Captain Bonneville to stimulate his recovery. A speedy recovery was important to the Indians in the village, especially the medicine man. The Indians in the village considered it bad medicine to have a white man as a guest in their village and the medicine man wanted Captain Bonneville's stench out of his tent. It was common for Indians of the plains to dislike the way white men smelled.

It was decided by the village council that the white man must leave as soon as he was fit. I was not told this in so many words, but I perceived that the members of the village felt that I and my children must leave soon as well because if this man had traveled so far to find me, others would surely come also. This could endanger the members of the village.

My brother and Little Feet did not want us to leave, but my brother had a position of responsibility within his village and he had to agree with me that it was best if my children and I left. So, it was decided that in the spring of 1834 that my children and I would be escorted by a small contingent of braves west to the Bighorn Mountains and Captain Bonneville would be escorted east to the nearest army fort. Captain Bonneville left first. No one in the village showed any remorse at his leaving. They all seemed very glad to see him and his bad medicine depart. If he was grateful for the medical attention he had received over the last nine months he did not show it. He seemed as glad to depart company with the Indians, including my brother and me, as we were to be rid of him.

I never saw Captain Bonneville again. Sometime later, however, I heard that he had returned to Washington to brief his superiors on his mission in the west and that he was reinstated in the army. It should be noted that some historians believe that he was never actually given a leave of absence at all. This would explain why he had been able to have a fort built, manage an unprofitable fur business, order expeditions to California and the Oregon territory, and pursue me across the Bighorn Mountains with a band of Indians in tow. This would also explain why he had always been, excepting short assignments, posted in Washington and why he was later to become the secret advisor to President Jackson on Indian affairs. Apparently Captain Bonneville had had the continuous, full backing of President Jackson during the entire time of his so called leave of absence from the army. He must have been some kind of secret agent assigned to protect the secrets of the government of the United States.

Chapter Ten

Chief Father of Many

Shortly after Captain Bonneville left my brother's village my children and I made plans to leave as well. However, we were delayed because of a message we had received from another branch of the Omaha tribe. We were told that the chief of a small village was an old acquaintance of mine and he had news about a huge French mountain man by the name of Joseph Chouinard. This was startling news to me because for the last three years I had assumed that the father of my children was dead. I was thinking: could this huge mountain man be my Joseph? Equally perplexing was the news that this chief, whom I was supposed to have known, was said to be half Negro and half Cherokee.

I found it hard to believe that Edward Rose was alive and well somewhere in this same area and that he was a chief among the Osage Indians. I agreed to stay on at my brother's village until further word was received from Chief Rose. A few months later I received word from Chief Father of Many, Mr. Rose's Indian name, that I was invited to his village for a visit. I agreed to come but without my children. I did not want to part with them but I also did not trust Chief Father of Many since he had almost raped and killed me the last time I had been in his company. My brother's father-in-law agreed to allow five braves from his village to accompany me to the Osage village and to ensure my safety. The chief of the Omaha village was also somewhat distrustful of the half Negro chief whom he had never met, especially because he was half Cherokee.

I soon found out that Chief Father of Many deserved his name. He had a small harem of four wives and had fathered 17 children in less than five years. Sometime later on in the night after Joseph had conked him on the head and we had left him for dead, two Osage squaws, with whom he was already acquainted, had transported Mr. Rose away from the Popo Agie River Rendezvous and nursed him back to health. He later repaid them and two of their sisters as well by protecting them and providing for them after the fashion that an Osage woman is accustomed. His prowess at fathering children and his expertise as a hunter and warrior gained him great respect in the small village where he resided. Consequently after the old chief died, he was the unanimous choice to be the new chief. The Indians in his village prospered during his tenure as chief and his particular brand of mixed blood was considered to be good medicine among these Osage Indians.

When I arrived at his village, Chief Father of Many greeted me with apparent enthusiasm and gave me many gifts. He later apologized profusely for his actions on the night of the Rendezvous five years earlier. In tears he told me that he would rather have died a thousand times himself than have harmed a single hair on my head. He told me that alcohol was a poison to him and his kind and, although he did not partake of it often, once he had taken one drink of whiskey he became a wild animal that was helpless to control its consumption. He also related that when he was in this state he could not control himself and became a slave of his primal desires, with no more ability to control himself than a stallion pursuing a mare in heat. In addition, Chief Father of Many told me that he had always loved me like a daughter. In fact, he had sworn to my own father that if anything happened to my father, Mr. Rose would watch over me, protect me and care for me like I was his own daughter. He then told me he would never forgive himself for failing so miserably, but he hoped that I could someday forgive him. Finally, he also related that he no longer held any animosity toward my large Frenchman for conking him on the head because he knew he deserved it and swore he would conk himself on the head if he thought it would set things right between us.

It was a hard thing for me to do, but I had been through so much with this man and I knew that a good friendship like we had once had was very hard to find in this western wilderness. So, I allowed him to hug me like he used to when I was a child of 13 or 14 with too many secrets and too many enemies. It felt good and I vowed never to deny myself or this man that simple pleasure in the future unless, of course, he had been drinking. He said he had never tasted whiskey since that night at the 1830 rendezvous and never intended to again.

I had made my peace with Chief Father of Many and I was rewarded with information about my Joseph. The chief told me that Joseph Chouinard had left the rendezvous and went into hiding for a time because he feared that Mr. Rose would come looking for him and kill him. Joseph was no coward but he knew

Mr. Rose's reputation. Mr. Rose's ability to hold me down on the night he almost raped me several years ago was no accident. He did, in fact, have superhuman strength. He had been a Strong Man in a local circus in New Orleans in his younger days and he had been a professional bare-fisted boxer as well. He had actually killed several men with his bare hands during some of his bouts. His drunken escapades were also legendary, and it was said that if you ever wronged him he would track you down and kill you slowly. These things about Mr. Rose my Joseph already knew and they would be told to me sometime later.

Chief Father of Many had, in fact, tracked down Joseph but he had not killed him. He had thanked him. However, Joseph had become a drunk and a wild man himself by that time. He also had garnered a reputation—his drunken rampages were also legendary. He would go on benders for several days at a time and soon earned the reputation as "the Bully of the Mountains". I did not know any of this information then, and even though the chief knew it he was not the kind of man to talk derogatorily about another man—especially to the mother of the man's children.

Even if I had known this information then, I still would have wanted to see Joseph and tell him about his children. The chief told me he no longer knew Joseph's location but he said he was certain Joseph was still in the fur trapping business. He believed Joseph still attended the yearly rendezvous because that was the best and maybe even the only way available to an independent trapper to dispose of his furs.

After my visit with my old friend, Edward Rose, I decided I should return to my brother's village and collect my children so we could continue on our original path to the southwestern foothills of the Bighorn Mountains. Arriving at this spot had been my ultimate goal every since my father had told me so many years ago what should be waiting there for me. As I said before, I had memorized the map he had given me although I had never been in the exact place shown by the X. I knew however, that the location I sought was a small cave in a canyon about two miles from its southern entrance.

I had never really been in a hurry to get to this canyon before because I knew the secret was safe, but I was now being drawn to it with an intensity I did not fully understand. It was like I had a subconscious sense that the secret was now in danger of being revealed. I knew now that at least two other people knew that something of great value was hidden in the Bighorn Mountains. I also knew that I and anyone close to me would always be in danger because of what I knew or because of what they thought I knew.

I, of course, now had another reason to go back to the area south of the mountains. The next mountain man rendezvous in the summer of 1835 was scheduled to be in Green River, about 200 miles southwest of my canyon, and I expected the father of my children, Joseph, to be there. Now that I knew his last name, I assumed he would be easier to locate, that is as long as he was still alive. I knew however, if I was going to find Mister Joseph Chouinard I was going to have to hurry because it was already late spring, and even with Indian escorts and good horses it would take my children and me and my old pack mule more than two months to make the trip. At the time I did not know it would actually be many more months before I would set eyes on Joseph Chouinard, nor did I know that when we finally met again he would be a very changed, and in fact, a very strange man to my would-be adoring eyes.

Chapter Eleven

West Becomes East

My Indian escorts and I took our leave of Father of Many and his people and traveled east toward my brother's village as fast as we could ride. However, *Wakonda* (the Great Mysterious) seemed not to be in harmony with us. We soon heard rumors and saw signs of renegade soldiers dressed as Indians in the area. It was further reported by some Indian scouts in this area that these white men were pursuing a "big half-breed" woman and her "bastard twins".

As we got closer to the village, scouts from our party confirmed our greatest fears. The village had been burned to the ground and many of its residents slaughtered, women and children alike. Those who could fight had fought their white foes valiantly, but because many of the fittest braves were escorting me across the northern plains the few warriors present in the village at the time of the attack were no match for their assailants. After I received this news from our advance party and was told there was no sign of my brother or my children, although his wife, her father the chief, and the medicine man had been killed, I knew the blood was again on my hands. My presence and the presence of anyone associated with me was enough to endanger all who came in contact with us or who may know our whereabouts.

My pursuers were ruthless. I did not know what I should do. ty children, my brother, and his children were missing and ere was no sign of where they may have gone or whether they had escaped on their own or had been taken. The only thing to do was to pursue the attackers, and by so doing hopefully find my children again. This pursuit would certainly delay my reunion with Joseph, but my return to Green River and the reunion seemed less important at that time.

We spent some time looking for signs that would lead us in the right direction. Eventually we found a trail that had been left by at least ten heavily laden beasts of burden, including my old mule. The absence of the mule and certainly the fact that the mule might be in the possession of my pursuers potentially presented another problem for me as well. The map that was so sorely wanted was sown under the skin of this mule. Even though it was located in a place that would not easily be detected, I could not be sure I had not been observed during the act of fixing the map there since the then seemingly incoherent Captain Bonneville was present at the time. More important however, because of the many deep tracks we had found heading toward the west, it became apparent that my children may be with the attackers, for the party was too large and the beasts too heavily laden to be made up of my brother and the four children alone. My children had most certainly been captured and were in grave danger. Even though they were, in fact, innocent it might be assumed they knew information about my whereabouts and/ or my secret and they would probably be questioned or even tortured sooner or later. We needed to find them without delay. We were probably not a large enough force to overwhelm their capturers but we had to try.

After several days of avid pursuit we found my old mule, which apparently died of natural causes or simple fatigue, lying beside a thicket of scrub brush. The skin under its belly had been opened by a crude object—perhaps a sharp stone and the map had been removed. I was thinking: could this mean that the map had fallen into the hands of the pursuers of my secret and they were now in a mad dash for the area where the map could lead them? If so, my children, if they were actually with the party we were tracking, were in even greater danger. They were no longer needed as hostages. The treasure seekers had what they thought they needed and might simply kill my children and any other hostages and leave them behind on the trail.

There was one thin line of hope that tugged at my heartstrings. The evidence that a crude instrument had been used to remove the map from the hide of my dead mule suggested that the posthumous surgery had been performed with something other than a knife. Any and all the white men in the party we now pursued would certainly have possessed a knife. My hopes lay in my belief that my brother or one of the children had performed the operation and removed the map. Whether their possession of the map was good or bad for them, at this point in time I could not know, but it still gave me some hope that they were and would remain alive.

Two days later along the trail we found a dead horse that had been butchered and partially eaten. The blood had even been drained and had probably been drunk. This indicated that the party was probably low on water and low on food and would be slowing because they had two less animals to carry themselves and their other burdens.

On the fifth day of our pursuit we found human footsteps, both large and very small alongside the hoof prints. This meant that some of the children were alive. Other signs told us we had nearly caught up to at least some of the people we pursued. I became desperate in my pursuit. I realized that if the men were starving and suffering from thirst and hunger the children would be in gravely poor health by now.

We soon caught up to some of the party we were pursuing. It was dark and they seemed to be holed up behind some large rocks—possibly under an overhang or even in a small cave. We could hear their voices—desperate voices. The men were bickering. The children were whimpering. I could not tell how many men nor how many children were there. The men would be weak—maybe unable to put up much of a fight. We were also weak and weary, but my adrenaline flowed. I knew I would be a fierce foe in a fight at that moment but we must be cautious. In an out-and-out open battle the children would undoubtedly be harmed if not killed.

We made our plans and waited. We had the advantage. I was accompanied by a fine bunch of Indian warriors and I was very much like an Indian warrior myself. I was a woman, sure but I was taller and stronger than most men and I was burning with the motherly need to free my children from the human beasts who held them captive.

We decided we would mount a stealthy attack shortly before dawn. Very slowly and warily we slithered into position and waited. I could hardly contain my desire to pounce upon these vermin and slit their throats even while they slept.

Finally the sky in the east began to lighten ever so slightly and it was time to act. I could see the forms take shape in the dim but growing light. I found I was able to discern between the human-shaped lumps under the blankets. Some were prone. Some were sitting. Some were small. Some were larger. The time to act was at hand. If we waited another minute we might lose our advantage.

I had long ago mastered the skill of taking life without making a sound, but the need to kill and kill again without making a sound had never seemed more necessary to me than it was at that moment. The lives of my children and my comrades in arms, not just my own life, depended on my skill—first the hand under the chin to stifle the death scream—then the sweep of the razor-sharp knife. Make it deep from ear to ear. Lower the body softly to the ground in the same motion. There, it is done. Then I took the next one. That was two. I knew that at that same moment at least three other attackers were doing the same as I. The absence of any sound told me they were also successful. It was nearly done. Then I heard the report of the pistol and I was on the ground, but amazingly I was still alive and I felt no pain. How could this be?

It was now becoming light and I could see my brother lying on the ground with a large, growing red shape on his chest edged in black. The image I saw could only be blood encircled by a short-range powder burn. My brother's glazed, nearly lifeless eyes stared up at me and there was a slight smile of triumph on his lips. I had saved his children and mine and he had given his life to save me. It was a bittersweet moment for me but it was short-lived because my children began to scream and call out to me from under the nearby dwarfed and twisted pine tree to which they were tied. My motherless/fatherless niece and nephew were there as well. The four of them were a beautiful but pitiful sight. I could easily see they were very near death and in need of immediate care, plus they were in shock from the sight of the eight dead white men whose throats we had so gruesomely cut and from the sight of their dead uncle/father. What was there to do? We had to attend to them but we also had to leave this place. The pistol shot and the subsequent scream of the soldier as his skull was caved in by one of my companions in retaliation for the shooting would most probably bring more white soldiers or hostile Indians to the scene.

Although we had to leave the children needed some sort of refreshment right away before we could begin our journey. They needed warm food but because of their weakened states, they could not consume solid food. One of our seasoned warriors assessed the situation and immediately provided a solution. With a rifle butt he conked one of the starved, exhausted horses on the forehead just between its eyes, just hard enough to render it unconscious. Then he made four small slits along one of its rear thighs. The four children were carried to the back of the horse and left to suck the blood that slowly flowed from the wounds. This was a macabre scene to observe even to the most seasoned warrior, but the blood quenched the children's thirst and renewed their strength enough to enable them to travel to where we could make a proper camp, cook some food, and rest.

We put the spent horse out of his misery by administering another blow between it's eyes, gathered up what livestock, guns, and other useful objects such as were lying about, and took our leave of the dead soldiers. We traveled just far enough on that first day to get to a place where we could protect our camp from all sides and build a small fire without it being observed. Although water and game were scarce in the area between the two outposts (later to be called Torrington and Sundance) one of the braves found a small reservoir suitable for watering our stock and for our own drinking and another brave was able to kill a couple of rabbits. The water was alkaline and it tasted terrible and the two rabbits were not much of a feast for six adults and four children, but the water and the meat would keep us alive and give us enough strength for the next day's journey.

The air was hot, but as we headed southeast the grass became more plentiful and our animals regained some of their strength. Two more days of travel brought us back into the lands of the Omaha. I knew that my children and me were bad medicine to the Omaha people, but according to the customs of these braves I had with me, we had to return to provide my brother a proper burial and to respectfully mourn the loss of the chief, his daughter, and especially the medicine man who had died at the hands of the whites.

At the time I never really thought about it much, but in this year of 1835 the Indians of the Great Plains began to transfer their war-making ambitions away from their ancient Indian enemies and focus it toward the white intruders. And it was a different kind of ambition. The Indians respected their Indian enemies and did not fear them or hate them, nor did they wish to completely destroy them. They made war on them sometimes to take revenge but more often to steal livestock and acquire slaves. They did however learn to fear the white men and their atrocities and they did not respect them. The white men seemed to have no honor in the way they made war—how they slaughtered women and children apparently for sport. Even the dreaded taking of the scalp was learned from the white men.

Until the arrival of white men in large numbers to the Great Plains the Native American never knew fear or hate, nor did they worry about the future of their kind. Even then, in the early years of the white man's domination of the Indian nations, some forward-seeing wise men among the Indians sensed it was the beginning of the end for "human kind". The ancient ways, the good old ways, the ways of living that had been passed on from generation to generation for more than 30, 000 years, were changing. The Indians knew what was necessary to become and continue to remain human beings—what rules one must live by. The Indian elders saw these rules being broken by the white men and soon some of the Indians would begin to break these rules as well and become as the white men—less than humans. The end of the Indian world, as they had always known it, was near. That is what the Indian began to think in 1835. Soon they would know.

Finally we were back in the lands of the Omaha and we came upon a moderately large village. I would not enter with my children. We made a small camp in a place I considered to be a safe enough distance away to prevent our bad medicine from endangering the people there. While my children rested and regained their strength I observed the traditional burial and grieving ceremonies from afar. Because of the status of the deceased Indians and the fact that an entire village had been so brutally wiped out, the activities lasted several days.

Eventually, the Indians got to the part of the ritual ceremony when they vowed to avenge the destruction of the village and the death of its inhabitants by killing as many white men as they could in the future and in as cruel a way as possible. Finally, the activities were over and I was ready to depart. Although my twins and I were not provided any escorts this time, I was provided with three fresh young mules and ample supplies including what crude weapons the Indians could spare.

Chapter Twelve

West to Destiny and Demise

We were again on our way northwest toward the Bighorn Mountains and toward the canyon and the cave. However, it was late summer by then and the Rendezvous was over. I was thinking that I would never see Joseph again and my twins would never meet their father. Had I known what would happen to us in the next few years, I would probably have headed east back to St. Louis instead and tried to forget that Joseph Chouinard, and the cave and the canyon and the map and the gold had ever existed. However, hindsight is always better than foresight, so I headed west with my little incomplete family toward our destiny and toward our nearly complete demise.

We followed the Platt River west—leaving the land of the Omaha and entered the land of the Sioux. I did not fear attacks by the Omaha or the Sioux because they knew me and I knew them. The Omaha were my mother's people and my father and brother had lived among them. My father had also befriended and lived among the Sioux and I had fought on their side against both white men and other Indians. However, there were other enemies around. There were the Crow and the Anadarko, and the Blackfoot, there were the renegade, lawless, white soldiers, and there were my ever-present pursuers from Washington.

Because of my increasingly poor eyesight, I could not see these enemies that lurked in the shadows along the trail but I could feel their presence. I could feel another presence as well. The Omaha had not provided me an escort per se, but they were with me nonetheless—observing from a distance. And there was also someone else out there waiting for the right opportunity to make his presence known.

I did not know it then but my old friend Mr. Rose had a vested interest in making sure that I reached my destination safely. Initially he had protected me for all these years because he believed he had a right to half of the gold buried in the cave in the Bighorn Mountains, but he no longer cared about these material things. At the moment Joseph Chouinard conked him on the head Mr. Rose became a different man. He realized who and what he really was. He was a man of honor committed to upholding the promise he had made to a friend. He was a man who wished to remain dedicated to a cause he had committed to long ago—a kind of special patriotism. He had also come to know himself not as a man driven by greed to obtain material things, but as a man driven to fulfill his sexual desires. Edward Rose realized on that day, at that moment, in 1830 that nearly everything he had done up to that time he did to fulfill this desire. He had become a strong man so he could put himself in a position to gain sexual favors; he had become a pirate, a smuggler and a thief to get the money to pay for sex; and he had even, perhaps subconsciously, stayed by my side and protected me—watching me grow into a woman in order that he could some day have sex with me.

Chief Father of Many now had at least four wives who he could have sex with whenever he wanted and his wives wanted him too. It cost him nothing. He had no need for the white man's money he had spent so many years of his wasted youth trying to get. In addition, he was getting older. He was 64 that year and his priorities in life were changing, even though he did not wish to admit this to himself. So, he followed. He followed me at a distance so he would be detected neither by me nor by my pursuers, but he followed nevertheless. He now felt that he had two purposes left in his life—protect the girl and protect the document. Before I continue to relate the facts about our trip back to the Bighorn Mountains and to the canyon I will tell you about my secret and the five other men who wished to keep it or wished to expose it. It is time.

Chapter Thirteen

The Secret

Prior to 1762 the French had possession of all land, in what was to become the continental United States, west of the Mississippi River except the Southwest, and the English possessed all land to the east. The area that was later to be included in the Louisiana Purchase passed to Spain in 1763 after the Seven Years War and was later given back to France in 1800. However, this return of land was kept secret until 1803, shortly before it was purchased by the United States.

In 1795 Spain granted the now-independent United States use of the harbor in New Orleans and unrestricted rights to navigate the entire Mississippi River. This was very important to the new nation because imported and exported items traveled in and out of New Orleans from and to international ports and up and down the Mississippi. However, in 1798 Spain revoked those privileges without giving a reason.

The reason for this change of heart by the Spanish government was known to only a handful of people. Officially only two members of the Spanish government and two members of the British government were supposed to know the secret but the secret was known to at least four others. I know at least these other four people knew the secret because two of their names and their special seals were affixed to a document; and the other two stole the document and the money that was supposed to change hands between England and Spain. These other four people who knew the secret were Thomas Jefferson, then the Secretary of State of the United States; Paul Barras, the main executive leader of the French Directory regime; my Father Manuel Lisa, at the time a freelance spy and smuggler who had previously worked for the governments of Spain, France, and even England; and a Mississippi riverboat pirate by the name of Edward Rose.

Just prior to the closing of the Port of New Orleans to American traffic in 1798, there had been an agreement made between England and Spain for the purchase of *all* lands west of the Mississippi River for a sum equivalent to 20 million US dollars. This agreement was profitable to both sides. It gave England control of the Port of New Orleans and the Mississippi River, which would put a stranglehold on America's re-supplying capability and her ability to trade with Europe. Also it would stop the United States from trading with the far western outposts of the continent. Spain would receive 10 million dollars in gold coin, which would strengthen her ability to trade on all fronts and allow her to block France's attempt to establish a French empire on the American continent. The other 10 million dollars would be in the form of war materials, which Spain could use to defend itself against the Americans and the French. The money was to arrive at New Orleans from England in a British ship flying a Dutch flag, be transferred to a Spanish ship flying a Dutch flag, and be taken back to Spain. How the British got ahold of 10 million dollars in gold coin I do not know, but I do know that this transfer of wealth was the reason the Port of New Orleans and the Mississippi River had to be closed to all other commerce in 1798. This is part of the secret that my father told me on his deathbed. He also told me that he had stolen the money and hidden it. I did not find out until much later that Edward Rose was involved in the theft as well.

Thomas Jefferson was, as I said, aware of this arrangement and he also became aware that the money never made it into French hands. The most important thing to him was the rumor that the document with his signature on it as a representative of the United States, also had been taken and was believed to have been transported to the western wilderness along with the money.

Ten million dollars was a lot of money in 1798; it was a lot of money in 1835; and it is a lot of money now, but the safeguarding of a document—a secret agreement between representatives of four nations that seemingly would benefit only two of these nations, was to die for. Many men died to keep this document secret and many had died and would die in order to expose it. Sure, some men were motivated to find the gold, but this was purely greedy self-interest. The document was different. The entire political establishments of four different nations could have been reduced to rubble if this document had been exposed to the general public. It would be the greatest international scandal of all time.

From the moment Thomas Jefferson heard that the document might have been stolen along with the money, the recovery of this document became his secret quest until his death in 1826. This is because he had the most to lose by its exposure. Once he had become President of the United States and Louisiana had been purchased from the French, Jefferson confided in his personal secretary and longtime friend Captain Meriwether Lewis. He did not tell him the entire story. He did however, tell Lewis about the ten million dollars in gold and that a document, if found, should be directly returned to Jefferson without being looked at by Lewis or any of his men. It was for this reason (to find the document) that Jefferson commissioned the Lewis and Clark Expedition and the reason (the recovery of the money) that Lewis and Clark agreed to go into the wilderness. Clark and others led several other expeditions into the wilderness on behalf of President Jefferson but Jefferson never did discover the exact location of the document or the money; and, although he was born into one of the richest families in the American Colonies, he died broke. He did however, before his death, pass on this secret to one or more members of a secret society he had been a member of since his college days.

As I said, the gold coinage and the document arrived at the port of New Orleans. The coinage was supposed to be transferred to a Spanish ship and transported to Spain, and the document, which was in a diplomatic pouch, was supposed to be taken directly to the American Secretary of State Thomas Jefferson for safekeeping. My father Manuel Lisa and another smuggler and river pirate, none other than Edward Rose, were at the port and were prepared to preempt the transfer. Since their smuggler's barge was docked close by, they were able to transfer the coinage and the document to their waiting barge and ferry it north on the Mississippi River to St. Louis and northwest via the Missouri River. Then they traveled overland via South Pass into what is now Wyoming Territory. Historians believe this pass was not discovered until the 1820's, but they also state that my father did not keep a record of his travels. It is also generally recognized that the Indians and early independent trappers and traders were aware of and used passes through the mountains long before the Lewis and Clark Expedition.

My father and his small party headed north to the foothills of the Bighorn Mountains and my father hid the money and the document in a small cave in a place now known as Crazy Woman Canyon (named after me). Later, he drew a map on birch bark which details the exact location of the coinage and the document. The site where my father hid these items has never been excavated, but the map is still in my daughter's possession and our secret will be passed on to future generations. I have no doubt that future members of the Executive Branch of the United States government will continue to try to uncover the money and the document. Our family's struggle to keep these items hidden may continue for generations.

You may wonder why I am not willing to turn over the money and the document to its rightful owners. The reason is that I believe that the money was made while Britain was involved in the Golden Triangle which involved the buying and selling of slaves. I am confident this money will be needed for some good cause in the future. Until that time, the descedants of Manuel Lisa will keep the money and the document safe and they will have help. I personally do not think that revealing the document would be prudent at this time. Maybe sometime in the future mankind will be willing to accept what the conspirators on all sides did and why they did it and forgive them. As long as officials of ours and other governments are willing to kill in order to keep this secret we can be sure that mankind is not yet ready to accept a truth such as this.

Chapter Fourteen

The Guardians of the Secret

Thomas Jefferson was an idealist and a dedicated scholar and wished to be remembered as such. He had no desire to attain further wealth. In fact, he despised his wealth and he despised wealthy merchants and others who wanted to fill their coffers by exploiting the new United States' location, natural resources, people, and opportunity to trade with other countries, in order to gain more wealth. The only advantages that his personal wealth held for him was that it provided him with the resources to pursue his scholarly and idealistic quests. It also provided a certain amount of power, prestige and respect. A poor man in his era would not have been able to rise to the political heights he did and would not have had the opportunity to study the philosophies and political systems of other countries, let alone draft a Declaration of Independence.

Thomas Jefferson was certainly no expansionist. He would have deemed a nation very much larger than our thirteen original colonies as being so large as to be unmanageable under the form of democracy that he advocated. I am not certain why he supported the agreement and affixed his signature to the document I have spoken about, but I am fairly certain it had something to do with stifling this westward expansion that would later become our Manifest Destiny. However, Thomas Jefferson was smart enough to know that it was better to go down in history as the president who advocated the colonization of the western part of the American continent rather than the traitor who sided with England, especially during the period in our history between the War of Independence and the War of 1812. This is why he felt he needed to get that document back at all costs and safeguard or destroy it.

France, after the revolution and Robespierre's rein of terror, was in turmoil. By 1798 however, France had achieved a certain amount of stability under the Directory. Paul Barras became one of the members of this new form of government and was supported by Napoleon Bonaparte. In return for that support Barras nominated Napoleon to be the commander of the French Army and helped facilitate Napoleon's marriage to Josephine de Beauharnais.

The money France had hoped to use to finance her secret plans to establish a North American empire was nearly depleted. Barras probably thought by signing the agreement that he would gain a lasting peace with England and Spain. He needed this peace with England and Spain because he wanted them to sign a treaty that would give Louisiana back to the French.

It may seem bizarre that Barras would sign such an agreement that allowed the Spanish to sell Louisiana to the English but he apparently had his reasons. Perhaps he felt that he could kill two birds with one stone. Since this was a secret agreement and the purchase was also to be secret and if the money the English paid never reached the coffers of the Spanish, the British war-making machine would be weakened and no transaction would take place. Furthermore, if the Spanish could be blamed for the disappearance of the money, Britain would more likely go to war with Spain rather than France, therefore France would be free to reacquire Louisiana and sell it to the wealthy new American nation.

As I already mentioned, Barras had the backing of Napoleon Bonaparte, who was not only one of the best battlefield strategists of all time, but was also an adept political strategist as well. Barras, however, must have realized that openly signing such an agreement would not look good for him. I am not certain as to why he signed it himself, but I assume that was the only way he would be able to keep it secret.

Secrecy would become even more important in the early part of the next century because certain events were pushing France and England ever closer to war with each other. This need for secrecy became very important because the money did, in fact, come up missing, the British Empire was, in fact, weakened by this loss of funds, and the British did eventually sign the third Treaty of San Ildefonso allowing France to take possession of Louisiana. The signing of this treaty seems odd since France and Spain had signed a treaty a few years earlier agreeing to be allies against England.

Obviously, there was a lot of political intrigue during and after the turn of the century and Barras and Napoleon were right in the middle of it. Eventually, Barras' alleged public and private immorality became his downfall and he may have brought the Directory down with him—allowing Napoleon to become the first Consulate of France. Although Barras was interested in keeping the document and his involvement with the agreement to allow England to acquire Louisiana a secret at the time, after his downfall Napoleon did not really care if it became public. He felt no need to pursue the lost money or the document. He, of course, had bigger fish to fry.

The English and Spanish officials had obvious reasons for signing the agreement and wanting to keep it secret. The English did not want anyone, including their own citizens to know they were willing to dispose of such a large sum of money or even how they got it in the first place. They also did not want anyone to know they were willing to contribute to Spain's war-fighting capability, especially the citizens of the United States and the citizens of France. Spain, of course, did not want the agreement to become public because of their alliance with France. The exposure of an agreement allowing England to purchase Louisiana, an area that France wanted to acquire through treaty especially when Spain and France were allied against England at the time, would have been very detrimental to the supposedly friendly relationship Spain had with France.

Neither the Spanish nor the English were concerned about the loss of the document because they did not know it was lost. The American Secretary of State was supposed to safeguard it and he never told Spain or England it had been lost. The French, as I mentioned earlier, knew about the loss of the document because they had a hand in the theft of the money and they knew the document had been stolen as well. My father was working as a spy for the French at the time and they provided him with the information that allowed him and Mr. Rose to get hold of the money and the document and transport it up the Mississippi that had been closed to other traffic by the Spanish.

My father, Manuel Lisa, had stolen the money because he had apparently wanted it for himself and he had stolen the document because he apparently knew he could make a lot of money selling it to those who wanted it destroyed. He also had apparently intended to blackmail those who wanted the document kept secret or had intended to sell it to those who wanted to expose the scandal. As an active spy and smuggler, my father knew how to barter and knew who would pay top dollar. Unfortunately, the same people who he had expected to get richer by exploiting had had him killed before he was able to derive any benefit from his theft. My father was already a very wealthy man but he was a very greedy man as well and he paid the price for that character flaw. Edward Rose had different motivations for taking part in my father's caper. He was not a schemer like my father and he had his feet firmly enough on the ground to realize he could not swim in that big of a pool. So, he had no interest in the document. He just wanted his share of the money. He thought that even a small percentage of it would be enough to meet his needs. He dreamed of residing in a first-class brothel where he could have his pick of beautiful ladies whenever he desired them. He even dreamed of having his own harem. As I mentioned before, he eventually got his harem and it never cost him a cent.

Chapter Fifteen

Reunited

My twins and I and our protectors and pursuers continued to move along the trail westward into the land of the Sioux. My daughter had had enough presence of mind, even at the age of four, to use a sharp rock to remove the map from the underbelly of my old mule after it had died, and she had somehow been able to do this without being detected. When we rescued her from her captures she had it in her possession. I had not realized she had seen me sew the map under the mule's skin nearly a year earlier—she was a very observant three-year-old and, luckily for us all, she was up way past her bedtime on that fateful night.

My pursuers had apparently decided not to attack or capture us. I have to assume they felt it more prudent to have me lead them to the money and the document rather than try to take the map from me and find the stuff themselves. Perhaps this was because Captain Bonneville had convinced their superiors that the map did not exist after all or that it had been destroyed. In any case, I hoped that I had seen the last of that old soldier.

It took a lot of time and the going was tough but we were able to reach the place where the Powder River crosses what would later be called the Bozeman Trail, in an area that would eventually be northern Wyoming, before the first snowfall of 1835. This spot, which would later be called Crazy Woman Crossing, is the location where I decided to build another trading post. I decided to do this because I was ready to settle down with my children with or without a husband. I had already had experience at running a trading post and, even after all I had been through since I abandoned the fur trapping and trading business, I still had enough money to buy the essential items to stock my trading post. What else could I do? I was a 26 year old mother of two with poor eyesight, arthritis, and several joints that refused to bend completely or to completely straighten out. I had no prospects for a husband and I had lost all hope of finding one in this western wilderness. Yes, I had again given Joseph Chouinard up for dead.

I was soon to find out that, in fact, my Joseph had sustained a serious injury at the hands of another mountain man and he was at the time I was building and stocking my trading post very near death. It was in this condition and under these circumstances that he eventually came back to me.

In the early spring of 1836 a much-changed Joseph Chouinard walked in to my trading post and promptly passed out. I did not recognize him at first, but he was certainly a man in need of immediate medical attention. So I all but dragged his long thin, sick body into my trading post. I still do not know how he found his way there, but once I started nursing him back to health and realized who he was, I knew it was time to return the favor and save his life. It was not an easy task. He was very thin—almost starved. He had a high fever that refused to break and he had gangrene in his right hand. There was not a doctor around for at least 100 miles and, even if I could have located one and managed to bring him to my cabin, Joseph would have surely died before I returned. My only option was to liquor up the man and saw off his hand to stop the infection from spreading and causing his death.

I boiled some water, sharpened and disinfected an old meat saw as best I could, built a fire and heated up an old forged iron poker I found, forced a large quantity of pure whiskey down the unfortunate man's throat and some down mine for good measure, and commenced to sawing on his wrist. I could have saved some more of the whiskey for myself for afterwards if I had known that the coward would pass out as soon as I touched his bone with the saw. His unconscious state did make the operation easier. I commenced to cutting through his bone and the rest of the meat, grabbed the poker and cauterized the wound with it, dressed the wound, cleaned up the mess I had made in my cabin, and let the poor devil sleep.

Wakonda, you should have heard that poor man scream when he woke up. I struggled to keep Joseph alive for the next few weeks. His fever finally broke and he was able to eat solid food again in a month or so. After a few more months, he had made a full physical recovery. Unfortunately, his emotional scars ran deep. I did not find out the extent of this emotional pain or what caused it until later. I assumed that his need to consume mass quantities of whiskey whenever it became available was entirely due to the frustration of losing his hand. Since I had been the one who actually removed his hand I was able to abide his bouts of drunkenness, at least at first. We eventually got married.

It seemed like the right thing to do at the time since he was the father of my children and I felt an obligation to take care of the poor desolate creature.

My new husband Joseph stayed drunk when he could, which was not as often as he would have liked because he would not abide anything other than Taos Lightning and supply trains did not yet stop in this place as often as they would in later years. During the times he was sober and even sometimes when he was not he talked about how we came to meet again after all these years. The following account of this is based on what he told me and what I was later able to piece together through other sources. Certainly my new husband's version of what happened was less lengthy and probably less accurate than this one.

Chapter Sixteen

The Famous Fight over Singing Grass

The famous mountain man Kit Carson was born in 1809. So, Kit, Abraham Lincoln, and I were set upon this earth in the same year. I never met Mister Lincoln neither did I know Mister Carson. However, my husband certainly knew Kit because my husband Joseph Chouinard was also a mountain man and he and Kit were involved in a fight over a beautiful Navaho woman called Singing Grass at the 1835 Rendezvous at Green River in an area that would later become southwestern Wyoming. This fray with Kit would change Joseph's life forever and would send him on the path which allowed us to be reunited.

Mr. Carson's memoirs state that my late husband was a hothead—a cowardly cuss always spoiling for a fight when he had enough alcohol in his gut to make him brave enough to take action. Joseph held a similar opinion of Kit except that Kit was no coward. Joseph claimed that Kit's small stature caused the pipsqueak to be incapable of backing down from a fight, and since he fought often, was very good at it and also very lucky. Mr. Carson had his version of the story and Joseph had his. Some historians have stated that Joseph, also known in those days as the Bully of the Mountains, wanted to bed Singing Grass. It seems that Kit Carson wanted to do the same and that Singing Grass preferred Kit to Joseph. Joseph reportedly went on a drunken binge, insulted Singing Grass and tried to rape her. Later he insulted Kit Carson and they decided to fight. They both got on their horses and pointed their loaded and cocked pistols at each other at close range. They both fired at the same time but Kit's luck prevailed when Joseph's horse jumped when he fired, causing him to miss. Kit's bullet found Joseph's thumb and blew it off. Historians suggest that Joseph Chouinard must have died from his wound because he was never heard from again.

In any case, it was the wound to Joseph's hand and the wound to his pride that caused him to ride north from Green River and leave the life of the mountain man behind him. Soon afterward the near extinction of the beaver in North America which led to the subsequent extinction of the mountain man, Kit Carson became a guide for the Army and rode in the many campaigns to rid the west of the Indians of the south west and the Northern Plains. Joseph Chouinard, as I already stated, got married and became the co-proprietor of a trading post at a place that would later be known as Crazy Woman Crossing.

Chapter Seventeen

The Trading Post Near the Canyon

Joseph Chouinard traveled north to a place where a trail, which later became part of the Bozeman Trail but was already well known to the Indians, traders, trappers, and the army scouts many years earlier, crossed the Powder River. This place was near the mouth of a beautiful canyon, had a good water supply, adequate quantities of small and large game for hunting, and enough timber and sod for building. It was at this site where the children and I built our trading post and established trade with the Indians and other people who happened along the trail or lived within one or two days' ride of the south entrance of my canyon. Yes, I call it my canyon because I considered it to be mine even before it was named after me.

After Joseph recovered his health to some degree he still chose to stay at the trading post, supposedly in case anyone wandered in either to buy, trade, or possibly even plunder it. I believe the true reason was that he wanted to stay there and drink when he had some whiskey or stay and wait for the supply wagon to bring some when he did not.

It was up to me to fish, hunt, and forage in the canyon. The canyon was breathtakingly beautiful in all seasons. The walls were of nearly solid rock and I had to look almost straight up to see their highest points even when standing in the middle of the canyon. There were no roads or structures of any kind in the canyon at that time—only a narrow footpath along the creek distinguishable only by the tracks and droppings of the animals that used it. So, I only had to share my canyon with the various creatures that inhabited it and an occasional trader, trapper, or Indian.

Because I was well armed and not recognizable as a woman in my buckskins, all manner of human beings who I met in my canyon gave me a wide berth. The creek itself was narrow but deep and clear. It was so clear that I could see the beautiful trout that shared the creek with the waterfowl and other plants and animals. Although the trout were quite plentiful they were difficult to catch for the same reason that they were easy to see.

The many rocks that had fallen down from somewhere up above during some ancient tremor of the earths crust enhanced the grandeur and the magnificence of the creek and the canyon floor. Mere words cannot adequately describe this spectacular gift of nature, so I will not try. One must see it for one's self.

Chapter Eighteen

Selling Whiskey to the Indians

Things went fairly well for Joseph and me and the twins for the first two years after Joseph got well. I, of course, was not able to completely forget about what was supposed to be in the cave in the canyon but I dared not go near the cave for fear I would be detected and give away the location. I also had another reason for putting my secret out of my mind. I did not want my husband to find out about the money that was supposed to be hidden there. I had seen how the lust for gold could change a man and Joseph had enough problems just trying to cope with his comparatively mundane life without becoming obsessed with finding a treasure.

Perhaps this was a foolish hope, but I hoped that the four of us could make a life for ourselves here in the wilderness. It seemed that our trading post was in an excellent location and I firmly believed that soon traffic through the area would increase and we would again have a good business. Joseph was a good husband most of the time and kind enough to the children and me. He did seem to suffer from excessive mood swings on occasion, which were hard for the children to understand. Later

I learned that this was a characteristic of most serious alcohol abusers.

Joseph was easy to get along with when he had a bottle as long as he did not get too drunk, but he got increasingly harder to live with when he did not have one. When business got slow and supply trains began to come less often, he became angrier and angrier. When a trader who possessed some whiskey did arrive after a long dry spell Joseph had the tendency to withdraw from us completely and drink one or two bottles straightaway.

The last great rendezvous was in 1837. As you can imagine, business was very slow at our trading post after 1838. Business would be very good at this trading post in later years when wagon trains started using the path that would later be called the Bozeman Train. However, this would not be for another 25 years or so. We only had the occasional trapper coming in rather than the booming business of hundreds of industrious mountain men that I had witnessed during the heyday of the American fur trapping business.

Mostly we were bartering with Indians. If things would have continued in this manner, I am not sure how our lives at the crossing would have turned out, but an event that triggered a chain of other events disrupted our lackluster but fairly peaceful existence. A wagon loaded with Taos Lightning had come to the crossing. The entrepreneur who owned the wagon had traveled from New Mexico en route to the Oregon Territory. He planned to sell the highly-sought-after Taos Lightning to the saloons in San Francisco at a huge profit. It was a hazardous, foolhardy trip to make on one's own and the man, because of poor navigation skills, somehow ended up at our crossing instead of South Pass. He was nearly starved and his horses were nearly dead but his cargo was intact. He had certainly stopped at a place where his only cargo could be appreciated.

While the man recuperated my husband helped himself to several bottles of the strong whiskey and went on a drunken binge for more than a week. Two weeks later, after the entrepreneur had fully recovered, he apparently wandered off into the wilderness and was never seen again. His wagon full of whiskey remained parked next to our trading post. It appeared that we were now in the whiskey selling business with no one excepting the nomadic plains Indians to sell it to. Joseph did not mind the lack of customers at first. He was happy to drink the stuff himself. However, even the huge Frenchman with his huge appetite for whiskey got tired of drinking alone after a while.

Some weeks after the original owner of the whiskey wagon disappeared an Indian of apparent high stature visited our trading post. He soon noticed that our shelves were amply stocked with whiskey and asked if he might have a free sample. He had apparently developed a taste for whiskey when he had spent some time at a United States Army fort while negotiating a treaty. It had already become a common army practice to ply Indian chiefs with alcohol during negotiations of a treaty. The army negotiators had long since realized that given enough to drink the chiefs would agree to almost anything and even sign documents without bothering to find out what they meant. Such was the trust that the Indian had for the Great White Chief in Washington in the early days of western colonization. The chiefs naturally became even more trusting after consuming a generous amount of whiskey.

Joseph was aware of this abuse and the fact that whiskey seemed to have a more disastrous affect on the Indians than it had on persons of European descent, but he allowed our most recent guest to drink his fill anyway. Once the chief had traded everything he had on his person excepting his clothes for whiskey my dear husband threw him out and told him not to return without bringing much wampum with him. I think Joseph knew the Indian would be back as soon as he could. One drunk can guess the mind of another.

Some weeks later the chief was back. He was, as my husband knew, willing to give everything he had for more whiskey. This insatiable thirst for whiskey was becoming more and more common in Indians who had had any more than a cursory exposure to the white man's world. From the beginning of the colonization of North America by the Europeans the Native American Indian has been driven from his ancestral hunting grounds by force, through promises made to him, and through payment of money and goods of all kinds.

When the Indians would not leave the lands that the European American wanted to possess they were, very often, murdered in mass by the use of firearms, swords, and even diseased blankets. Very early in the nineteenth century the white leaders in Washington embraced an Indian dehumanization and an Indian extermination policy. However, because the new nation was supposed to have been built on God's principles, some religious and humanitarian groups began to protest against the atrocities levied on the Indians.

The white leaders in Washington still desired to exterminate the American Indian but, in order to appease these humanitarian groups, the leaders decided it would be more prudent to obtain Indian lands through treaties. These treaties, of course, were designed to obtain the Indian lands while giving the Indians very little in return. Because of this, some treaty negotiators began to ply Indians with alcohol to cause them to become more cooperative. This worked very well and it created in some of the Indians a dependence on alcohol that would eventually cause them to lose touch with their traditions, and over time, significantly contributed to their near extinction. The white leadership of the United States had no problem with this because the Indians had, to a great extent, been dehumanized and ultimately, as I have said, the extinction of the Indian was what was wanted.

It has been said that out of all the methods the white man used to destroy the Indian, the introduction of alcohol worked the best. However, getting the Indians drunk could sometimes backfire on the whites. Our case was but one example of how drunken Indians could get out of hand and "bite the hand that feeds them", as my husband said.

When the Indian chief came back he did in fact, give everything he owned in exchange for our whiskey. After all his possessions were in the hands of my husband, the chief was promised that if he brought other Indians to the crossing to trade he would, in turn, be given for free as much whiskey as he could drink. Upon drinking his fill, the chief left and soon returned with several braves who soon developed a dependency on the strong Taos Lightning as well. Joseph provided his ill-gotten whiskey to the braves for a modest price at first but once their dependence for the stuff was well established, the price was raised dramatically.

Soon my husband owned all of the possessions of this once proud group of braves. Since I was often in the nearby canyon hunting and foraging, I am not sure of the exact details of what happened to cause the seemingly docile group of Indians to become hostile, but I assume that it was because they had nothing more to use to pay for the whiskey and they were addicted to it.

One afternoon, after spending nearly all day in the canyon, I came back to our trading post and witnessed the following scene. The whiskey wagon was burning and my unfortunate husband and my two children were tied to stakes that had been driven in the ground. As I approached, I could see that under and around the stakes dry brush had been placed and some of this brush was already burning.

Chapter Nineteen

Pain was My Salvation

After the afternoon that I mentioned before, I became known, for a time, as Devil Woman or Crazy Woman. In former times I was known as Manuela Lisa and Manuela Chouinard but that seemed a very long time ago and my memories of that life had become clouded—perhaps because I, subconsciously, suppressed the memory. I became Crazy Woman to the Lakota and Crow because of the extremely bizarre behavior which I displayed whenever I was in their presence.

When I awoke I sensed it was mid day in early summer because I felt the sun, which was high overhead, warming my face and my near naked body. I could not see the sun. I was blind. I felt the leaded fists of panic beating upon my breast and the jagged teeth of insanity gnawing at my brain. Was I insane? I think not. I was enraged and I was in shock but insane—no. I had played the part long enough to know. Again—the panic, then I began to remember how I came to be called Crazy Woman. It was when I was forced to watch my husband, my son, and my daughter being burned alive by a band of drunken Sioux.

My eyesight was already very poor and getting worse all the time due to a conk on the head that I received several years earlier, as I have mentioned before, but I lost my sight completely after I saw my husband and children tied up and being burned by that frenzied group of Indian braves. That night I was literally blinded by rage. I was but loosely tied and the adrenalin produced due to my rage allowed me to tear myself free of my bonds and spring upon my tormentors with great effect. I could not see the Indians but I lashed out at them brandishing a burning pole, which was apparently used to support one of my children as they were being prepared to be burned alive. I was oblivious to the pain from the burning stake and I was also oblivious to the blows from the Indians I was attacking. I felled many and I heard their screams.

Although I was unable to actually see the results of the mayhem that I wrought, it was enough to disperse the band, enough to earn me my name, and even enough to ensure I would never be attacked again by any of the original inhabitants of the lands between the Black Hills and the Bighorn Mountains. These Indians are a superstitious lot and believe it is bad medicine to torment or otherwise have contact with one who appears to be insane or possessed of evil spirits. I was rid of the danger of attack by the Indians who coexisted with me in this rough and rocky canyon in which I was living. But still, I was blind.

I had survived through two winters and two summers and it was no comfortable period. I had little shelter other than the rocks, shrubs, and caves of this canyon and I had little to eat excepting the roots I could uncover and the insects I had found to eat. Now and then I also found some fairly fresh fish or meat thanks to my keen sense of smell that seemed to have become keener since I lost my eyesight. This food I thought at the time was apparently left for me by some well meaning Indian to keep me from starving. Water is plentiful in my canyon and I could melt snow for drinking in the winter. Fortunately I came to know my canyon well when I was still able to see so, I had little trouble finding my way around in it. My canyon, which was of a length I could cover on foot in a summer day, was only about a hundred yards wide at its widest point and much of that was taken up by the stream that ran down it.

Because of my blindness, I dared not leave the canyon that I knew so well. My life then was not much of a life at all but only a meager existence and I am convinced that I was only able to survive at first because I was in constant and excruciating pain from the burns and the other wounds I sustained when I assailed those who killed my family. This pain kept me alive. It made me hard and it made me sane again. For many months I woke up screaming from a sleep—nee a stupor, brought on by exhaustion from that same screaming, only to scream again. Such was the pain from my undressed wounds. This screaming did however, re-enforce to any would-be assailants that I was still possessed of devils—that I was still the Crazy Woman of the Canyon.

But no, I was never really insane. I know what insanity is. I have seen it in the eyes of trappers, hunters, would-be settlers, and other wandering folk throughout the years of my long life. Hunger can make one insane. Pain can also, but my pain did not. To be insane is to lose touch with reality. My pain was real. My pain was my reality. My pain was my constant—my anchor. Even so, I found the pain hard to live with.

I wished for death a thousand times a day but I could not take my own life. I could not pray to God for death or for the pain to leave me, for I did not deserve God's mercy. We, my husband and I, had forsaken God long ago. But I did pray to *Wakan-Tanka* (which I then believed to be the Spirit of the Canyon) and these were no silent prayers. I screamed these prayers just as I screamed myself awake in the morning and I screamed myself to sleep at night. I also prayed to *Wakonda* (the Great Mysterious or Great Spirit in the Omaha and Osage language) to forgive my red tormentors for they were drunk when they burned my family members at the stake. They needed that whiskey that drove them mad on that day and many other days and we, my husband and I, made them need it. In fact we destroyed the lives of this small band of renegade Indians, and other white whiskey peddlers destroyed the lives, families, and hopes of many others like them. Once the Indians near my canyon had tasted our strong whiskey they could not hunt or care for their squaws. They could only drink and raid and rape. They were lost, and we deserved what they did to us for we made a small fortune from their debauchery and their misery. We received our just desserts for they used some of that very precious but then plentiful drink to ignite the bodies of my loved ones. My husband and my children burned bright because the vile liquid was one hundred proof.

I'm not certain why European-born men can consume relatively large amounts of alcohol without suffering any ill effects, but the Indians could not. Even the ancient Aztecs recognized that alcohol was poison to them. They forbad those less than seventy years of age to consume it except on special ceremonial occasions.

So, I prayed—I screamed.

> Oh *Wakan-Tanka* stop my pain.
> Take my life tonight.
> For my deeds I deserve to die and burn in hell.
> Take my life tonight.
> I have ruined my red brothers—brothers who treated me well.
> Take my life tonight.
> I destroyed my red brothers—now destroy me.
> Take my life tonight.
> My greed has ruled me—I deserve no mercy.
> Take my life tonight.
> Come and cast your thunderbolt.
> Take my life tonight.
> Stop my pain.
> Stop my pain.
> Take my life.
> Take my life.
> Oh *Wanka-Tanka* cast your thunderbolt and scatter my soul to the four winds.
> Stop my pain.
> Stop my pain.
> Take my life.
> Take my life.
> Oh *Wakan-Tanka*, take my life tonight.

I screamed this prayer or one similar to it a hundred times a day for months but I did not die. The Indian spirits seemed unwilling to use their sacred powers to take my life. So, I wandered through my canyon—my domain, blind and without hope for many seasons. For a time, I forgot about the map and the money and the document. I temporarily forgot about my pursuers. I temporarily forgot about my Indian friends and my dead brother and my protector. I just about forgot about my father and his secrets and nearly even forgot about my dead husband and my dead children.

One day, about two years after my family had been killed my physical and mental pain and despair became so great that I felt I might actually be able to take my own life. I climbed up the side of the canyon in a place I remembered was not too steep for climbing and where there were large rocks below. I figured if I sprang headfirst from this point I would surely break my neck and die. So, I scrambled up to what I determined to be a sufficient height and tried to jump. Just when I was ready to dive to my death however, I lost my footing and slipped—tumbling head-over-heels down the side of the canyon. My fall was finally broken when my head hit a large rock rendering me unconscious for a time. I am not sure how long I was out, but I sensed it was dark when I came to. When I opened my eyes I experienced something extremely odd to me. I closed my eyes again but when I opened them for the second time I could see shadows. It was dark but I could see something.

I lay awake all night hoping to see something more, but the sky was apparently overcast because I could see neither the stars nor the moon. It was nearly pitch black but still I could see something. Finally, I fell asleep and when I awoke I could not only feel the warmth of the sun—I could see it. I sat up with a start. I could see other things too. I was no longer blind. Not only was I no longer blind I could see clearly. I could see the rocks and the stream. I could see the clear water there and I could even see the fish. I could see the spots on the fish and I could see them clearly. I could see the birds in the sky not only just hear them, and I could see the flowers on the hillside that were so far away I could not yet smell them. My vision seemed to be as perfect to me as it was when I was a child. I felt like a little girl again. I forgot about my pain for a time. I even seemed to be oblivious to the new cuts on my limbs and face and the new knot on my head. I skipped and ran about and jumped and even tried to do a cartwheel—such was my joy at regaining my sight and regaining it so completely.

I suddenly realized that, despite the physical pain I was to suffer acutely for at least another month and suffer to some degree for the rest of my life, I wanted to live. I wanted to live again. All of the sudden, it did not matter what had happened to my family and my friends as much as it did before. I was alive and I could see again. I began to scream again but these were not screams of pain or grief. These were screams of joy.

Whatever manner of man or beast that may have heard my screams, if he could think at all, would certainly have thought I was quite mad indeed. I was not mad—no, at least not anymore. Now that I could see, I knew that my knowledge of herbs and other homeopathic substances would allow me to eventually cure my wounds and stifle my pain. Yes, I could gather these ancient traditional Indian remedies again and I could prepare them properly as well because now I could see. I could see. I could see. Praise *Wakan-Tanka*, I could see.

Apparently, the Indians who shared this canyon and the nearby plains and mountains with me had been observing me for some years. They had observed me at my trading post during my frenzied attack on the drunken Indians who tied up and burned my family. They had seen me maim and kill several of these Indians. The Indians had also observed me while I was wandering in my canyon and bathing in my creek. They had heard my screaming and my praying and they had observed my fits of rage and frustration, my attempted suicide, and even my recent skipping, jumping, and frolicking. They had long since begun to refer amongst themselves to the location of my former trading post as Crazy Woman Crossing, to my canyon as Crazy Woman Canyon, and even to the creek that runs through that canyon as Crazy Woman Creek.

The Indians later observed me curing myself with herbs and other medicaments. This I had learned during my days in the mountains and during the period when I worked with the medicine man in my brother's village while he was tending the wounds of Captain Bonneville. The Indians who observed me after I had regained my sight soon began to realize that I could see—that I was not blind after all and this they must have found very bizarre and it must have strengthened their opinion that I was not a normal woman. Although they observed me with new respect, the name Crazy Woman would be my name as long as the Indians were able to pass this story on to other Indians who dwelt close by. Neither the Indians nor the white men of future generations will know the specifics of how it came to be, but they will always know that the places where I had blindly maimed and killed Indians and roamed around blindly screaming and praying throughout 1840 and 1841 would continue to bear the name of Crazy Woman.

Chapter Twenty

Medicine Woman

Some months after I regained my sight and my wounds were nearly healed, an Indian brave approached me. I had recently seen him and other Indians on the ridges and walls of the canyon but none had ever approached me before. I soon found out this was not just another Indian but a member of the Sioux tribe and one of my half-brothers. In addition, I realized this was the same brave who had looked so familiar to me, so many years ago, when he led the other mountain men and me through South Pass into virgin trapping territory.

I was not aware until that time that I had any half-brothers or half-sisters other than those evil white girls back in St. Louis, but I soon found out that my late father had bedded if not wedded several Indians maids of several different tribes during his long forays into the western wilderness.

The Indian brave knew who I was and he was able to perfectly describe my father. It seems that my father talked fondly of me with his Indian lovers and these lovers passed this information on to their children. My half-brother, Sleepy Eye, got his name from the fact that he was born with one lazy eye and the eyelid was always drooping down and covering it. My father had the same malady. That is why Sleepy Eye looked familiar to me back in the days that I trapped beaver with the mountain men and lived with and fought against the Indians. Sleepy Eye was glad to see me, although I certainly was no pretty sight since I was scarred by burns and other wounds. However, Sleepy Eye had not come to my canyon for a social call.

Sleepy Eye had a young wife who was due to give birth to twins but something was not right and it appeared to the women in his village that the birth could not take place in the normal manner. The village medicine man had died recently and there was no one else for Sleepy Eye to turn to for help within a day's ride. I soon found out Sleepy Eye and other Sioux braves had been tracing my movements since I came into their territory more than four years before and were aware of some of my trials and tribulations. They were aware I had given birth to very large twins on my own and had traveled all over the west with them in tow when they were barely able to walk. They were also aware I had saved my late husband's life by sawing off his wrist and cauterizing it with a hot poker. More recently, they had observed me regaining my sight and curing the infected open sores on my own body with preparations made from herbs that I had found in my canyon. Because of these things I had done for myself and others, my half-brother believed I had strong medicine and could help his wife when no one else could.

I was certainly willing to help Sleepy Eye's wife, but I had vowed never again to enter an Indian village because I still feared that any Indians who became associated with me would share the same fate as those in my late brother Raymond's village several years before. So, I decided to return to what was left of my trading post at the place that was now called Crazy Woman Crossing and have the pregnant Indian woman brought there. While I made my way to my old cabin that once had served as a trading post, my half-brother hastened to his village to retrieve his wife and the most experienced midwife of his village in case I needed help.

When I got to my cabin I found it in fairly good shape. Even the interior was untouched by the hands of man. Time and the animals—large and small—had taken a toll on it, but no human being had entered since the Indians had burned the whiskey wagon and subsequently burned my husband and children. This I am sure seems very odd to a white man or woman, but the Indians were a superstitious lot and they believed that there, within the walls of this small cabin, lived the spirit of the Crazy Woman. The Indians felt that *Wanka-Tanka* would bring bad medicine to them if they entered this place where the Crazy Woman once dwelt.

Sleepy Eye, being half white and also having little choice if he wanted to safe his wife's life, decided to enter my cabin with his wife. His wife was too weak to protest, but the Indian midwife refused to enter under any circumstances. Once I got the young mother-to-be inside I hoisted her up on a low beam which had been used to hang up deer to bleed out and which was the traditional birthing position of the Plains Indian. I soon realized however, that this was not going to work because the child that was in the position to be born first was breeched and would have to be turned somehow before the births of the twins could take place. Luck was with us that day because I had seen an old medicine man turn a breeched baby successfully once before. In this case the procedure would be complicated by the presence of a second child in the womb. All I could do was try.

The first thing I did was release the poor woman from the horizontal beam and then I placed her on the old table I once used to display goods for sale. Coincidentally, this was the same table where I had laid poor Joseph when I sawed off his wrist. This would be my second unassisted operation. The second thing I did was call on *Wanka-Tanka*, the Great Mysterious that is connected to all things both living and dead and both animate and inanimate to give me wisdom and skill.

Why should I not call on the spirit of the people of this place? I had suffered in my life as much as many shamans had suffered. I had nearly lost my mind and had certainly sent my soul on several voyages to seek the truth. I had always been honest about the things that mattered and I had treated the earth and all its creatures with respect and learned and performed the special rites required to be performed when it was necessary to take from mother earth in order that my family and I might survive upon her. I had taken what was needed and only that. The only exception to this had been when we trapped the beaver to near extinction. I could not help myself, brother beaver. This was the way of the mountain man. I have no excuse. I hope Mother Earth will forgive me and that *Wanka-Tanka* will help me now.

I had performed the required rites that the "Human Beings" had taught me as best I could and was ready. Time was of the essence, I could delay no more if this woman and her unborn children were to live through the next few hours. I had boiled some water and found a large bone needle similar to the one used by the medicine man I had observed turning a baby.

It worked and the first baby, a fine large boy, was born. Then the girl came out into the world. These were no easy births. The mother had already been in labor for many hours before entering my cabin, and it had taken several hours to turn the first baby and deliver the two of them.

When the husband heard the cries of his new son and daughter he ran into the cabin. In her excitement, the midwife followed. After that day, I became quite famous as someone other than a crazy woman. The name Crazy Woman, to the Indians in the area where I lived, became a term of endearment rather than just a name that represented someone who had exhibited bizarre behavior. After that day when my niece and my nephew were born, Indians frequently entered my cabin to socialize, barter with me and seek help when they were sick, wounded, or the sprits seemed not to smile upon them. They no longer feared that evil spirits or bad medicine dwelt there—just the crazy woman who performed miracles with the help of her good medicine, practical know-how, and homeopathic preparations.

I could not be known as a shaman because women did not hold that position in the culture of the Plains Indians, and I had not been purified in the sweat lodge nor had I smoked the sacred pipe. However, the Indians came to me in my cabin and sought my advice as they would have done if I were a true shaman. This arrangement was all right with me because I enjoyed helping these people and I loved the way they lived and the way they respected all things around them and all things that had come before them and all things that would come after them.

I continued living among the Indians but apart from them, as it was traditional for a shaman to do, for several years and I also reopened my trading post because travel through Crazy

Woman Crossing had increased over the last few years. It was 1850. I was 41 years old. I had been a mother—now I was childless. I had found my lost brother but now I was an only child again. I had been a wife but now I was a widow, but I had friends—the Indians and my half-brother who had a wife and two children who visited me often. I did not know it then but I also still had pursuers sent from Washington, but I also still had protectors. In fact, thanks to my old friend Chief Father of Many, all the braves of an entire Sioux village were dedicated to my protection and the protection of the gold and the document that lay in the cave in Crazy Woman Canyon. These treasures were quite safe, for these Indians had no desire to possess the white man's gold. However they would protect the gold and the document with their lives out of respect for the old chief and their now aging medicine woman.

My life among the Indians of the plains would remain peaceful for only about four more years. Ironically, by 1851 it seemed necessary to the white government in Washington to maintain peace in the west, actually to protect the growing number of white settlers from the savages who had been living on these lands for more than ten thousand years, by ratifying a treaty that gave the Powder River area to the Crows. This made no sense to the Crows or the Sioux or any other Indian who had inhabited the area. They did not believe in land ownership. The result was that the treaty and the boundaries were ignored. This treaty was seen as the beginning of the end of the traditional way of life of the Indians of the plains and the mountains. The increasing immigrant travel began to adversely affect the wildlife and the environment—endangering the livelihood of the Indian. These increasing tensions would soon lead to conflicts between the

Indians and the whites and between different tribes of Indians as well.

The major problem with this so called peace treaty and the others that came before and after it was that the white leaders in Washington did not really want to make peace with the Indian at all. They wanted to eradicate the Indian from the face of the earth. This eradication started in the east when it became necessary to push the eastern Indians farther west in order to make room for the increasing numbers of white settlers. It did not stop there however, the whites continued to press westward. Whenever the white men needed more land they would make a treaty that would give them that land, pushing the Indians further and further west into areas that seemed to the white men to be uninhabitable, but were deemed to be good enough for the Indian. Soon the white men would find a use for this "uninhabitable" land, break the treaty, kick out the Indian, and negotiate a new treaty. The white men pushed and pushed the Indian until there was nowhere else to go except to the arid plains between the Black Hills and the Bighorn Mountains. Starting in the 1850 the white men and their families even began to move through this land in increasing numbers on their way to the Oregon Territory. The Indians feared that they would lose this arid sanctuary as well and they became increasingly more hostile toward these travelers.

The first major open hostility between the Indians and the United States Government in the area that the Sioux considered to be their territory, even though it had been given to the Crow, was in 1854. Reportedly, a misunderstanding caused army troops to fire on a Sioux village but the Sioux had the upper hand in this battle and annihilated the army force. This, in turn, caused the army to retaliate over the next few years, but eventually the fighting stopped. Tensions between the army and the Sioux however eventually grew more intense and the Sioux and Cheyenne went even further west, and by 1860, forced the Crow out of the entire Powder River country.

Not long before 1860, the nomadic Indian tribes of the plains hunted and moved freely between the Black Hills and the Bighorn Mountains, but now their last free land seemed to be the Powder River country near the Bighorn Mountains. They were virtually surrounded by white men. The Oregon Territory, which was already heavily populated, was to the west and more and more settlers were restricting Indian movement in the east. The Indians were bound by the treaties enforced by the increasing numbers of army troops in the area. They had nowhere else to go. So the Sioux, with the help of the Cheyenne, vowed to protect their traditional hunting grounds. They fought valiantly to keep the traffic out of their area because they knew this traffic would eventually disrupt the fragile balance of nature and drive away the game by destroying their natural habitat. They never dreamed (actually some did) that white hunters would soon come and decimate the buffalo herds for sport and for the pleasure of wealthy whites, but this would come about very soon as well.

Chapter Twenty-One

The Bozeman Trail

The ancient southeast route that had been used by Indians for centuries and by some white traders and trappers was seen by the whites as a good way to connect the gold fields of Montana, near Virginia City, to the Oregon Trail in what was to become the Wyoming Territory. This route went right past the door of my trading post. By 1863, the route became know as the Bozeman Trail and the business at my trading post began to increase dramatically. Business would get even better over the next few years. However, my Indian friends became more and more agitated by the ever-increasing numbers of white travelers crossing their lands. The Indians even began to openly chastise me for trading with the white travelers—thereby providing them with the essentials they needed for their travels. The only thing that prevented a full-scale attack on these travelers was the fact that they were, at least during this time, just travelers. Very few whites were actually settling in Wyoming. They were moving on up the trail bound for somewhere else. In 1864 the floodgates seemed to open as John Bozeman led approximately 2,000 settlers up the trail past my cabin. Between 1864 and

1866 the Indians began attacking trains of settlers up and down the trail in a futile attempt to preserve their hunting grounds. These actions were self-defeating because the attacks on wagon trains caused the United States Army to build more forts in the areas along the trail to house more troops to fight off the Indians, thereby protecting the travelers. The army soldiers had superior fire power and would eventually defeat the Indians and force them to accept the presence of the white men in their area and accept the restrictive controls levied upon them as well. There was only one battle that took place in the immediate vicinity of my trading post between Indians and whites that deserves to be mentioned.

Chapter Twenty-Two

The Crazy Woman Battle

In July of 1866, just 11 days before my fifty-seventh birthday, a wagon train consisting of 37 people crossed the Crazy Woman Fork of the Powder River near my trading post. There were nine army officers, nineteen enlisted men and nine women and children. Two of the officers had ridden ahead of the train on horseback. This was a big mistake. Some of the Sioux and Cheyenne braves who were camped in the area had been spoiling for a fight for some time. They had observed wagon trains in increasing numbers crossing Crazy Woman Creek for several years, but out of respect for me and not desiring to harm too many women and children had not attacked any before. However, this was different. Two well-armed army officers were arrogantly crossing the Sioux hunting grounds without permission. This opportunity was too much to pass up especially since the leader of the Indian war party who was present that day had just lost his father and brother to just such a pair of officers as these. The Indians opened fire, hitting one of the officers and chasing the other one back to the wagon train.

The other officers were able to get the wagons circled before the Indians arrived at their location because the braves were celebrating the killing of the one officer they had hit. Apparently the officers did not feel that the position where they had circled the wagons was strong enough so they relocated to the top of the next hill. This action all happened very close to my trading post and I could see everything very clearly. During the relocation of the wagons and their passengers, I noticed that there were several women and children with the soldiers. When I made this observation, I ran toward the braves shouting for them to stop the attack at least long enough for the women and children to take cover. I did not particularly care if the braves attacked the soldiers or even held the women and children at bay long enough to cause the soldiers to surrender, but I did not want any women or children killed, especially near my trading post.

After several hours the people in the wagon train and the braves who had them surrounded saw dust coming from the north. Some of the Indians left their present battle to investigate. When they saw a lone soldier approaching in front of the cloud they shot him dead. When they saw that the dust was another approaching wagon train they decided to disperse and they disappeared into the hills. The Indians had gained a limited victory over the whites that day. They had killed two soldiers without any losses to themselves. However, this battle again reinforced to the leaders of the army that more soldiers were needed in the area to protect civilians traveling along the Bozeman Trail. It also convinced them that it had become necessary to either force the Indians onto reservations or completely annihilate "the vermin for the good of all decent Christian people".

After the Indians disappeared I went out to the wagon train to see if anyone was hurt and to offer the members of the two wagon trains supplies if they desired them. When I got closer to the first wagon train I noticed there was a woman with them who appeared to be in her mid-thirties accompanied by a twin boy and girl who looked to be 13 or 14. This woman had raven hair and was very tall and thin. She would have been beautiful had not her face been disfigured, probably in some sort of fire. She and her children were vary distraught and she kept trying to run out into the field to where the officer lay a few hundred yards away, but she and her children were being restrained by three of the other officers.

I probably would have recognized this woman right away if her presence there had not seemed so unlikely and she was in far too much shock from the loss of her husband to recognize me. After looking at the fine tall young man and the beautiful young girl at his side, I realized that these three travelers must be my daughter and my two grand children, but how could this be so? Indians had burned my daughter at the stake along with my husband and son many years before. Had they not?

Chapter Twenty-Three

How My Daughter Came Back to me

After a time, when my daughter Maria had calmed down, the other officers released her and she recognized me. We ran to each other's arms and embraced for a long moment. After the army officers were convinced there was no more danger of an Indian attack they released my grandchildren also and we all walked solemnly out to where the dead officer lay on the hard sunbleached ground. His scalp had not been taken and since he had been shot only in the chest very close to his heart, he had probably died instantly from the large caliber pistol and had not suffered. His tanned high cheekboned face stared up at us with open eyes. He had been handsome and had fathered two handsome children.

For my daughter and her two children, this was a time of mourning, but for me, although I understood Marie's sorrow at the loss of her husband and my grandchildren's need to mourn their father, it was also a time for celebration. I had thought my daughter was burned alive by drunken Indians 27 years earlier. I had never hoped that I would ever see her again because I was sure I would not. Now Marie had come back to me, and she had also brought me two beautiful Grandchildren. No matter what the circumstances, I was elated.

After a few hours of rest and replenishment at my trading post the officer who had taken charge of the two wagon trains decided it was time to continue north to Fort Reno. The body of Marie's husband would be taken there and after a short military ceremony, it would be taken overland by stagecoach to the nearest train depot and shipped by train to St. Louis. From there it would travel down the river by boat to New Orleans, and on by ship to Charleston, South Carolina, which had been the Lieutenant's home before the American Civil War, which we out west called the War Between the States. Marie and her children, Charles and Deborah, would accompany the body back home and I, not wanting to lose touch with my daughter and grandchildren so soon after finding them, decided to close up my trading post and travel east as well.

I had only been on a stagecoach once before and had never in my life been on a train, a large boat, or a ship. It would be a long trip, but it would give me a great opportunity to get to know my grandchildren and to get reacquainted with my daughter. On our way to Charleston Marie told me about her life since she had escaped from being burned alive by the Indians so many years ago.

According to Marie, on that day at Crazy Woman Crossing out side our trading post she had been tied to a post that had been driven in the ground by an Indian—she was only eight years old at the time. She stated that even though it happened a long time ago, she could remember it like it was yesterday. I was away hunting in the canyon and Joseph had been drinking with the Indians. There were six braves as far as Marie could tell and all the men were very drunk including my late husband, Joseph.

Everything seemed to be fine until Joseph refused to give the braves more whiskey because they had nothing more to trade for it. By then the braves knew the circumstances of how Joseph had taken possession of the wagon full of whiskey and they postulated, in their drunken states, that the whiskey was as much theirs as it was Joseph's. They tried to convince Joseph of this fact but he still refused to provide them with any more of the whiskey. So, one of them sneaked up on the big Frenchman and conked him on the head rendering him unconscious. My two children had tried to stop them but the Indians took several more bottles from our trading post and commenced to get very drunk.

After the Indians could barely stand they decided they would teach the big Frenchman and his family a lesson. They drove three fence posts in the ground and tied Joseph to one of them. When the children tried to stop them they grabbed up the children and tied them to the other two posts. The children started screaming at the Indians to let them go and shouted that their father would surely kill them when he got free. That is when things got out of hand. It started to get dark and two or three of the Indians lit torches. A couple of the other ones apparently thought it would be a good idea to put some brush up against the posts and pretend like they were going to burn Joseph and the children.

I'm sure these normally friendly Indians never really intended to set fire to Joseph and the twins. However, that is exactly what they eventually did. One of the Indians decided to throw some whiskey on Joseph to revive him, but after he had done this one of the torches got too close and Joseph was suddenly on fire. When this happened the children started screaming and whiskey was thrown on them also in order to shut them up. Somehow the flames reached them as well and the brush around my children started burning. The children began to scream louder but Joseph was still unconscious.

When I came running into the clearing near our trading post I saw three people, one large and two small, tied to burning stakes with at least six Indians dancing and yelping around the fire. I thought I was in hell. I went into a fury and rushed to the closest burning post and, with superhuman strength fed by adrenalin, I pulled the stake from the ground with the child still attached to it. At the same moment something snapped inside my brain and I became totally blind. I was oblivious to the pain in my hands from the burning pole. I was also not able to tell what had happened to the child who had been attached to it or even where I was in reference to the other two figures or the dancing Indians. All I could hear were screams as I lashed out blindly with the burning pole at anyone who seemed to be taller than three feet. I could tell when I connected with an Indian because he let out agonizing yelps of pain. I could not tell how many I had felled, but I continued wielding the pole like an enraged demon until all was silent and I had fallen down—exhausted.

When I could catch my breath, I tried to find my children and my husband but I could not find them in my blindness. I assumed they were dead and that the Indians had fled. I could smell charred bodies and the smell of death hung sickly sweet in the air. Soon my own injuries got the better of me and I lost consciousness.

Marie told me I had grabbed the burning pole that had held her to the ground and that she had been freed at that instant, sustaining burns only on her face, arms, and hands. She said that her father had never, as far as she could tell, regained consciousness before he was burned to death. However, she had seen her brother being burned alive that night and the sight of him and his screams had haunted her dreams all her life. She had been powerless to save him because of the flames that engulfed him and could only cower in a corner of the yard—watching her brother burn to death. It must have been a terrible experience for a young girl—even one who had been reared in the wilderness. Marie also said that I killed three Indians and she had clubbed one of the wounded Indians to death with a large rock. The other two escaped, dragging her along as a captive.

When the Indians returned to their village with Marie in tow, they were chastised by the chief for what they had done. Marie was taken into the village and placed under the charge of a childless squaw some forty years of age. She was treated well and raised as an Indian girl in that Sioux village which was near the mouth of my canyon. For the next ten years she was never allowed to venture away from the village without an escort. She had, however, heard rumors of a blind crazy woman who wandered through the canyon conjuring up spirits who protected and fed her.

Marie said she was very confused and scared during most of the time she lived in the Indian village. The Indians had been kind to her, but she was severely scarred both physically and mentally by the experience of nearly being burned to death by the drunken Indians, two of whom were still members of the village. She woke up screaming every night from the nightmare of seeing her twin brother burned alive.

Marie also told me at the time when her brother was being burned she thought that she could even feel his pain. Since then I had heard many twins claimed they could feel it when their twin was in pain. Some twins also have claimed to share memories with each other—a sort of telepathy. I was remembering then when my own brother stepped in front of the bullet that was meant for me and saved my life that I actually fell down and laid on the ground for a time clutching my chest as though I had been shot.

In some families like mine, non-identical or fraternal twins seem to be hereditary. I am not aware of whether or not my father or mother had a twin—my mother never mentioned it. I never knew any of my father's family and he never talked about any of his relatives. In any case, my grandchildren were at least the third generation of twins in our lineage. As I looked across the coach seat at my beautiful grandchildren I noticed how much they looked alike and how close they sat together. They seemed to be almost one person—of the same mind.

With great effort I pulled my glance away from the two sets of dark, mesmerizing eyes that belonged to my grandchildren and gave my daughter my full attention again. She was continuing her story. When Marie was 18 years of age, certainly old enough to marry in the Indian village where she resided, Indian braves had been looking upon her with mixed emotions for a few years already. She was a very tall woman and well built with slim hips and wide shoulders. Actually she was a head taller than most of the braves. Her face, hands, and arms were somewhat disfigured which kept her from being what one would consider beautiful, but her hands were dexterous, she was a good worker, and she was stronger than most men. Of course, one of the other physical traits that seemed odd to the Indians was her extremely large feet. Because of her disfigurement and her other physical peculiarities, the braves in her village were either unwilling or actually afraid to approach her. So, she remained unmarried. This was all right with her, she said, because she was still quite afraid of physical contact and because the trauma she had suffered at such a young age caused her to not fully trust any of the Indian braves.

Later on in her eighteenth year a young army officer came to the village. This was in 1848, several years before there had been large numbers of white soldiers in the area near the Big Horn Mountains. This particular officer was fresh out of West Point where he had studied the cultures of the American Indian. After he graduated he volunteered to serve at the army's most remote western outpost in order to see firsthand how the Indians lived and to learn their languages and customs. The Indians of this area were still very trusting of white soldiers at this time and they welcomed him to their village and allowed him to stay for some months. He was a very tall, dark, soft-spoken—almost shy man. His grandfather belonged to one of the old families in New York and his grandmother was of Huguenot descent.

When Marie first saw Army Lieutenant Napoleon Harry Daniels and heard him speak she fell head over heals in love with him. He had a smooth southern drawl when he spoke English, although neither the Indians nor my daughter would have recognized it at the time. Marie said, "His voice just sounded good—smooth and silky and sincere". Marie felt that although she was smitten with the young visitor that he could not possibly care for her—not in a million years, but it turned out that, in spite of her physical imperfections, he had taken a liking to her as well. He began to find more and more reasons to be around her and eventually to be alone with her over the next several weeks.

When it was time for Lt. Daniels, Harry as my daughter called him, to go back to the small fort where he was billeted, Marie surprised Harry, the Indians, and, mostly, herself, by agreeing to go with him. They got married at the fort shortly after and Marie gave birth to my grandchildren the following year. Harry's young family accompanied him to several army postings throughout the western part of the United States until early in 1861 when he felt obligated to return to his boyhood home of Charleston, South Carolina, to join the Confederate Army. Marie and her children went with him to Charleston and stayed in that once beautiful city until the War Between the States forced them to move further north. These were hard times both for the soldiers who fought for the South and for the civilians, especially the women and children, who lived there.

Harry's family was wealthy and his family, including his three sisters, youngest brother, and my Marie were able to avoid most of the hardships that would befall many of the other southern families, although they did suffer to a lesser extent and seven of the men, including Harry's father, eventually were required to fight for the South. Harry was the oldest son and he was the only one of the seven to be killed in combat, although one of his younger brothers died of typhoid fever during the latter part of the war.

During the first year of the war the South experienced several victories and it seemed that the differences between the North and South would be reconciled before too much damage was done. Both sides were initially confident that the war would not last long, and Marie and her husband's family believed they would be able to go home soon. At first the four young women and Harry's mother were involved in charitable activities. They eventually joined other young southern women who formed relief societies for the wounded soldiers and prepared winter clothing for them. Harry's grandfather also donated money to the war effort. He continued to do this even though Harry's family desperately needed the money themselves. This was typical of the old southern gentleman of the time, and it was necessary. The South Carolina Militia was not funded by the state or the government of the Confederacy such as it was. The officers provided their own clothing and much of their own food through allowances provided by their families. The soldiers from less affluent families very often depended upon clothing and food provided by these voluntary relief organizations.

By Mid-August of 1861, only six months after Fort Sumter was bombarded, beginning the hostilities, 20,000 troops were sick from typhoid or had been wounded in battle. One of Harry's brothers who was a doctor and was trying to obtain a commission in the southern army at the time, reported that the troops were still suffering from fevers and the field hospitals were being run by inexperienced surgeons who sawed off the arms and legs of the wounded soldiers and haphazardly threw them out of the doors and windows. He believed that many lives were lost due to ignorance.

Harry's mother, a well-educated and cultured woman and a very astute observer stated that by the fall of 1861, although she felt it was right that the South separated from the North, the war had ruined the hopes of her family. She feared that the five younger boys would miss their chances to obtain positions of prominence in South Carolina. Harry was a career officer and had already been promoted to Major since the war began but two of her other sons were only temporary Lieutenants, two had not yet received their commissions, and her youngest son, who was still in school, would surely not be able to complete his schooling because all males between the years of 16 and 65 would soon be required to serve in the army in some capacity until the end of the war.

By October of 1861 the Union flag had been posted in Georgia and South Carolina. Harry's mother stated that they now had "the flag of the enemy floating on their coasts". The town of Charleston was practically deserted soon after that. People were leaving their homes, burning their crops and burning their slaves' quarters. They either took their slaves along into the interior of the state or set them free.

Harry's parents and his grandfather had large plantations and kept many slaves. The parents possessed about 150 of the poor devils at the beginning of the war and the grandfather owned more than 200. The southern plantation owners considered their slaves to be part of their wealth and they certainly reduced the labor costs of growing cotton, tobacco, and other products that the southerners grew for sale. The slave trade was a lucrative business for all who were involved in it including the slavers, the transporters, and the plantation owners. There were also abolitionists who not only helped slaves escape from their masters but also helped provide shelter and transportation to runaway slaves as well as freedmen.

It was hard for me to understand how a family of persons could actually *own* other human beings but, although this was not acceptable to me, my daughter had no choice but to accept it and keep her thoughts about it to herself while living under her in-laws' roof. They had been brought up to accept the keeping of slaves as part of the southern way of life and would have been especially sensitive to criticism when this *right* seemed soon to be taken away from them. This possessing and buying and selling of these slaves, these unfortunate people of color, was to continue, to some extent, until after the War Between the States had come to an end.

By the end of 1861, Marie and the others felt that the bombardment of the town of Charleston was imminent and, although the plantation was on the outskirts of town, they were afraid that the burning and looting that had already started in the town would soon reach them. They packed up all their valuables, put their silverware in the bank, and prepared to evacuate. In May of 1862 my daughter and her in-laws departed from the nearly deserted city of Charleston and took up temporary residence in Spartanburg in a building belonging to St. John's College. They expected to be there only for the summer but ended up staying for the duration of the war. They finally returned to their plantation in Charleston only to find that due to the looting and vandalism during the war it was nearly useless. They had little money and little hope of restoring their family to the status they enjoyed at the beginning of the war. However, two of Harry's brothers did marry well later in 1866 and his youngest brother returned to college after only a year of military service. His father, his mother, four of his five brothers, two of his three sisters, and his wife had survived the

War Between the States that pitted brother against brother in the bloodiest war of our time. So, Harry's family fared much better than most southern families did but still they lost much of their property, their Confederate currency was virtually useless, and their southern way of life was much changed and rearranged. Eventually they might fully recover and the South might rise again, but I do not think it will happen in my lifetime.

Harry was a captain when he joined the army of the Confederacy and had risen to the temporary rank of colonel by the end of the war. He opted to remain in the United States Army and asked to return to the western territories. He was granted this request but, because he had served in the Confederate Army, was reduced to the grade of first lieutenant. Harry and his family, however, were very happy to return to the west and be posted in one of the most remote forts in the United States, Fort Reno in Wyoming Territory near the Big Horn Mountains.

Because of the numerous attacks by Indians along the Bozeman Trail a series of forts were built. Fort Reno, originally called Fort Conner, was one of these. It was built on the Powder River in August of 1865 after the end of the War Between the States. During the fall and winter of 1865-1866 a small group of ex-confederate soldiers were sent out west to man this fort. These soldiers were called Galvanized Yankees by the army leadership and the ex-members of the Union Army. It is doubtful that many of these Galvanized Yankees were volunteers and it is also doubtful that many of them took their families along to such a remote outpost. However, Harry did volunteer to go to Fort Reno and he did bring his wife and children along. They all felt more at home in this remote area of the west than they had in Charleston or anywhere else on the eastern seaboard.

Chapter Twenty-Four

The Indian Wars

After the Sand Creek Massacre there was considerable pressure in the eastern part to the United States to establish peace with the Indians and acquire free passage through their lands by negotiating treaties rather than fighting. This was important to the white leadership of the reunited America because since the Civil War was over and people could resume free movement within the United States, more people wanted to travel west up the Oregon Trail and then north up the Bozeman Trail to the Montana gold fields and the Oregon Territory. The negotiations with the Indians, which were held at several places in and near Wyoming Territory including Fort Laramie, may have succeeded except that at the same time the Eighteenth Infantry of the United States Army was detected by other Indians as the soldiers marched up the Bozeman Trail to build more forts. The building of more forts along the route was certainly not in the best interests of the Indians in the area and it somewhat soured the negotiations.

Chief Red Cloud, the leader of the Ogallala Sioux and one of the chiefs involved in the treaty negotiations at Fort Laramie, expressed his displeasure of the unauthorized troop movements across Indian lands. Red Cloud and some of the other Indian leaders, who were also opposed to the presence of Army troops in the Powder River country, traveled north and alerted the Sioux and Cheyenne. However, the long wagon train with supplies for Fort Reno and materials and tools to build the next fort up the Bozeman Trail continued on. These actions by the United States Army illustrate the single-mindedness and deceitful attitude of its leadership at the time. They wanted it to appear that they were willing to negotiate for peace with the Indians. What they really wanted, as I previously mentioned, was to make the Indian disappear from the entire United States. However, if this could not be done, they, at the very least, wanted to lock them away on some remote and desolate reservation where they could keep track of them and completely restrict their movements. If this was to happen it would be the end of the American Indian as we had known him.

The next fort the army built along the Bozeman Trail was Fort Phil Kearny. Soon after construction began it came under attack by Indians. Again these actions by the Indians were self-defeating because they caused the Army leadership to recognize the need for more troops to be sent to the area and still more forts to be built to protect travelers going up and down the trail. Soon Fort C. F. Smith was also built on the Bighorn River and this, in turn, perpetuated more Indian attacks. Soon the Bozeman Trail was closed to civilian traffic because travel was deemed by the Army to be too hazardous due to the large number of Indian attacks in the area. To me it seems plausible that the frequency and ferocity of these Indian attacks may have been exaggerated, and the closing of the important route to civilians could have been a ploy by army leadership in order to justify the construction of the forts and the stationing of more troops in the area. There were certainly enough troops available after the War Between the States because being in the army; even at a remote outpost, was preferable for some to living in the war-torn southern part of the United States and having to compete for jobs with all the other ex-soldiers.

The Indian leadership was certainly aware that the building of these forts greatly threatened their way of life and some realized that life, as they had known it, was nearly at an end. The Indians were hopping mad about this and they had also started using some American military tactics in their campaign to rid their territory of the white soldier. They began to try to lure the soldiers out of their forts where superior numbers of Indians awaited to ambush them. After two prior attempts, the Indians succeeded in December of 1866 and lured Captain Fetterman and 80 men away from Fort Phil Kearny and annihilated them with a force of hundreds of Indians. This was the worst defeat the army had suffered at the hands of the Indians of the Great Plains.

During 1867 however, there were only a few small battles between the soldiers and the Indians and, although the United States Army continued to improve the existing forts along the trail during that year, by 1868 the lack of traffic up and down the Bozeman Trail caused army leadership to decide that the forts were no longer needed and that they should be closed. In the fall of 1868 the Sioux and Cheyenne Indians finally had the Powder River country to themselves once more. However, the United States Army still intended to herd the Indians onto reservations even though the white population of the Powder

River country remained small. It is hard to understand why the American government took this stand against the Indians since it seems so unnecessary, unless one realizes that the government leaders were greedy and wanted the land solely for themselves and, of course, they still had that old original policy of completely eradicating the Indian from United States territory from shore to shore.

In 1876, after the Indians had enjoyed a somewhat peaceful existence in the Powder River country even though they were constantly being herded toward the reservations, the biggest clash between the army and the Indians took place along the Little Bighorn River. This was the largest defeat the United States Army has suffered at the hands of the Indians but it was the Indians' last hurrah. Soon afterward the last free-roaming Indians were defeated and forced onto reservations and the Indian "problem" was finally solved, at least as far as the United States' leadership was concerned.

In 1877, the Bozeman trail was again open to white settlers and they were free to establish farms, ranches and communities in the area of the Powder River. The era of the nomadic American Indian had come to an end. The proud, noble Indian of the plains with his vast knowledge of the world he roamed and his complicated rituals, rites and wonderful ecological practices was forced to live in the square houses that the white man had built for him. Living in these square houses he could no longer find his center and without his center he was lost. He had nothing left except his despair. He was finally completely ruined and without hope.

Chapter Twenty-Five

Home at Last

My late son-in-law, of course, did not live long enough to see the final defeat of the Indian. I often wish I had not. It was a sad time for everyone who had Indian blood flowing in their veins. My daughter, my two grandchildren and I, left Charleston soon after Harry's funeral and returned to the eastern edge of the Bighorn Mountains. Charleston was no longer the gem of a city it had once been, and Harry's family was devastated by the blow of his death out west. It nearly killed his father; his mother became depressed and remained in a state of depression and disillusionment until her death in 1881. My daughter was certainly grateful to have had the opportunity to live with her in-laws and remain close to her husband during the War Between the States, but she was not a southerner and her husband had never intended her to live in Charleston. He had always intended for his son to grow to manhood on the western frontier and for his wife and daughter to be able to enjoy this free but difficult life as well.

Since my daughter was a widow of an army officer we were allowed to stay at Fort Reno and we were provided with a small house within the protective walls of the fort. Later we moved on to Fort McKinney, which was the new fort that was built at a much more habitable location after Fort Reno was abandoned. In 1880 we all moved to the newly established town of Buffalo, which had sprung up near the new fort. That is when our fortunes took a turn—for better or for worse? I will let you decide for yourself. Your decision will be based on your moral convictions. I am beyond morals now, that is if I ever had any to start with. My father certainly seemed not to. Am I not a product of my upbringing? In 1880, I became the first proprietor of the Occidental Hotel, Saloon, and Brothel.

Seventy years of age may seem old to start a new business but one has to put meat on the table somehow. My daughter remarried and both of my grandchildren married as well. All six of them took advantage of the Homestead Act and collectively acquired a large acreage at the southeastern mouth of the Crazy Woman Canyon on Crazy Woman Creek. Of course they called their newly acquired property The Crazy Woman Ranch. Once they had lived on the land for five years, according to the Homestead Act, the land became their own. They prospered and their brood multiplied. My granddaughter gave birth to eight children over a period of ten years and my grandson had an even larger family. He fathered eleven children in that same period. Between my grandson's family and my granddaughter's family there were four sets of twins and one set of triplets. The triplets were identical. All three girls had bright red hair and green eyes. All the rest of the children had dark hair and dark almond shaped eyes.

One warm summer day I was sitting on the wooden porch of my hotel watching the slow moving traffic passing by on the muddy street in front of me when I saw a very old Indian with a great shock of white curly hair and very dark skin approach me. As he got closer, I noticed that he had a valise in his hand marked with a United States Government seal. I had never seen it before, but I instinctively knew that it was the diplomatic pouch that held the document my father and Edward Rose had stolen at the port of New Orleans 82 years earlier. Who was this messenger? Was it possible that this old dark-skinned Indian was Edward Rose? If it was, he was 108 years of age. It seemed impossible to me at the time and it still does, but it was he—Chief Father of Many himself. Historians have reported that Edward Rose died among the Indians in 1832, but he in fact lived to a ripe old age.

My old friend Mr. Rose struggled across the muddy street, walked directly up to me and handing me the pouch, said, "I will not see the leaves fall from the cottonwoods. This is your worry now. I suggest when you rebuild your hotel you build it out of brick and include a large vault so you can keep this document and your gold safe because I can not watch it for you anymore. The Indians are all defeated we can no longer protect your treasures. Our job is done." Then my old friend walked in to my saloon at ten o'clock in the morning on a Sunday and ordered whiskey. He drank several shots of my best in quick succession and then slowly slipped from the bar stool onto the sawdust floor and stayed right there. He was dead as a stone. I still have the pouch holding the document and the gold is still safe in my new vault. The secret, the document, the map and the gold will pass to my daughter after I am gone. However, my time was not yet up. I am supervising the construction of my new hotel, which will be made of brick, replacing the old wooden building. Of course, I had the vault built first. I would very much like to see this project through to its end, but I am over ninety years old and I am glad I was able to relate this story of my life and my canyon to my three beautiful green eyed great-granddaughters before passing on to the next world. What a treat to have spent one of my last afternoons on this earth telling my story to such wonderfully attentive youngsters. I hope I did not fib too much.

The End

CPSIA information can be obtained
at www.ICGtesting.com
Printed in the USA
BVHW08s0413080818
523859BV00003B/12/P